The Road Past Altamont

From Bill
Christmas 2003

The Road Past Altamont

by Gabrielle Roy

Translated from the French by Joyce Marshall

University of Nebraska Press • Lincoln

First Bison Book printing: 1993
Most recent printing indicated by the last digit below:
10   9   8   7   6   5   4   3   2   1

Library of Congress Cataloging-in-Publication Data
Roy, Gabrielle, 1909–
[Route d'Altamont. English]
The road past Altamont / by Gabrielle Roy; translated from the
French by Joyce Marshall.
p.   cm.
ISBN 0-8032-8948-0
I. Title.
PQ3919.R74R613   1994
843—dc20
93-14195   CIP

Reprinted by arrangement with Fonds Gabrielle Roy, Montreal,
Quebec, Canada. Originally published in French in 1966 under the
title *La route d'Altamont*. This English translation by Joyce Marshall
was published the same year by McClelland and Stewart, Limited,
Toronto.

∞

Contents

My Almighty Grandmother

I WAS six years old when my mother sent me to spend part of the summer with my grandmother in her village in Manitoba.

I balked slightly at going. My old grandmother frightened me a little. She was known to be so devoted to order, cleanliness, and discipline that you couldn't leave the tiniest thing lying about at her house. With her, it seemed, it was always, "Pick up after yourself, put away your things, as the twig is bent . . ." and other admonitions of the sort. As well, nothing exasperated her so much as the tears of children, which she called "mewling" or "caterwauling." That was another thing: her rather curious way of speaking, partly invented by herself and often far from easy to figure out. Later, however, I found several of my grandmother's expressions in my old *Littré* and realized they must date back to the time when the first settlers came to Canada from France.

Yet she must have found time heavy on her hands, for it was her own idea that I should spend part of the summer in her company. "Send the little sickly one to me," she wrote in

3

a letter my mother showed me as proof that I would be welcome at Grandmother's.

Those words "little sickly one" had already made me feel none too well-disposed toward my grandmother; so it was in a more or less hostile frame of mind that I set out for her house one day in July. I told her so, moreover, the moment I set foot in her house.

"I'm going to be bored here," I said. "I'm sure of it. It's written in the sky."

I didn't know that this was precisely the sort of language to amuse and beguile her. Nothing irritated her as much as the hypocrisy that is natural to so many children—"wheedling and coaxing," she called it.

So at my dark prediction I saw something that in itself was unusual enough. She was smiling faintly.

"You'll see. You may not be as bored as all that," she said. "When I want to, when I really set my mind to it, I know a hundred ways to keep a child amused."

But, for all her proud words, it was she herself who was often bored. Almost no one came to see her any more. She had swarms of grandchildren, but she seldom saw them, and her memory was failing, so it was difficult for her to tell one of them from another.

From time to time a car full of young people would slow down at the door, perhaps stop for an instant; a bevy of young girls would wave their hands, calling, "Hello, Mémère. How are you?"

Grandmother would just have time to run to the doorstep before the girls disappeared in a whirlwind of fine dust.

"Who were they?" she would ask. "Cléophas's daughters? Or Nicolas's? If only I'd had my spectacles I would have recognized them."

"That," I would inform her, "was Berthe, Alice, Graziella and Anne-Marie."

"Ah!" she would say, struggling to remember whether these particular girls were the daughters of Nicolas, of Cléophas, or of Albéric.

The next moment she would begin to argue with herself. "But no. What am I thinking? Most of Nicolas's children are boys."

She would go to sit for a moment in her rocking chair beside the window to try to settle the matter once for all and make a complete inventory of her descendants. I loved seeing her like this, looking for all the world as if she were unraveling some skeins of tangled wool.

"In Cléophas's family," she would begin, "there's Gertrude first, then the oldest son—now what is that big dark boy's name? Is it Rémi?"

"No, indeed. Now let's see," I would answer, beginning to lose my patience. "Rémi belongs to Uncle Nicolas."

"Ah, you don't say," she would remark with a vexed look.

But I noticed that little by little she became less troubled by my awareness of her infirmities—her dimming eyesight, her faulty hearing, and, what was even more irritating to her, the failure of her memory.

The following day another group of young people might descend upon us, this time by buggy, "but only for five minutes."

Grandmother would hurry to set the table, perhaps hoping to bribe them to stay, but nothing of the sort: the moment she had gone down to the cellar to fetch a pot of gherkins, the girls in their Sunday clothes would be caroling, "We can't wait. We're on our way to Rathwell. . . . Bye bye, Mémère!"

She would come up, blinking a little, and ask, "Have they gone?"

From outside could be heard a great racket of departure.

"Oh these modern young people!" Grandmother would exclaim.

We were alone in the little house, listening to the lamentations of the prairie wind as it writhed interminably in the sunlight, forming and re-forming tiny rings of dust.

Grandmother would begin to talk to herself, perhaps unaware that I was listening. One day I heard her sigh at the window.

"You're always punished by the very things you thought you wanted. I probably wished too often for comfort, to have everything neat and tidy, to be free of children clinging constantly to my skirts with their doleful wailing. I wanted just one minute to myself. Now I have a whole century to myself!"

She sighed again, then began to reproach God.

"Why does he listen to us when we ask for things that won't suit us when we get them? He ought to have sense enough not to listen."

Then she remembered my presence in the house and summoned me with a little gesture of the hand.

"Well, at least I know your name."

Then she asked, "And what is your name again?"

"Christine," I told her with some annoyance.

"Yes, that's so. I knew. Christiane."

And, lost in her thoughts, she asked, "And how old is that little girl?"

There was one time of day when I never failed to feel a sense of boredom and lassitude coming over me. This was the moment when the sun, just before it disappears, casts a great red light over the prairie, a remote strange light that seems to extend its vastness and at the same time empty it of all human presence, as if giving it over to wild dreams of the time when it existed in utter solitude. It seemed then that the prairie wished to have no people, no houses, no villages upon itself, that it had tried, with a single stroke, to rid itself completely of all this and be once more as it was in the old days, proud and lonely.

At Grandmother's, moreover, there was no way to avoid this disturbing sight. The village was small and Grandmother's house stood right at the end of it; the prairie surrounded us like the ocean on all sides except the east, where a few other little houses could be seen, our companions on what seemed to me a terrifying journey. For in the complete immobility of the prairie, one had the sense of being drawn forward on a sort of voyage across an endless land of everlasting sameness.

Suddenly, understanding neither my sorrow nor its source, I burst into loud wails.

"Oh I'm so bored, so bored, so bored!"

"Will you be still," said Grandmother irritably. "You make me think of a coyote howling at the moon."

I tried to be still, but soon my strange sorrow, nameless, with no cause that I could define, seized me again and I howled more loudly than ever. "Oh I'm so bored, so bored, so bored!"

"Ah, the poor Innocents!" said Grandmother.

This was always her term for unhappy children, especially when they were in the depths of their inexplicable distress. She might have been alluding to the Massacre of the Blessed Innocents—I do not know—but whenever she saw a child weeping bitterly she would exclaim, in an indignant voice, "Ah, the poor Innocents!"

In vain she offered me all the many good things to eat there were in the house, and finally, knowing no other way to distract and console me, she said, "If you'll just stop caterwauling, I'll make you a doll."

Immediately my tears stopped. I looked skeptically at my grandmother seated in her high rocking chair.

"You find dolls in stores," I said. "You don't make them."

"That's what you think," she said, and began as usual to complain about stores and high prices and the present-day custom of buying everything ready-made.

When she had vented her anger in this way, a little glimmer came into her eyes that I had never seen there before; it was quite extraordinary, like a light suddenly kindled in a place one had believed abandoned and overgrown. What she was going to accomplish today began, however, in the simplest way in the world.

"Go to the attic," she said, "and fetch my big scrap bag. Don't make a mistake. Get the one that's tied on top with string. Bring it to me and then you'll see whether I can make what I've a mind to make."

Still incredulous, but curious too and perhaps secretly hoping to catch Grandmother napping, I went in search of the big scrap bag.

From it Grandmother drew some bits of multicolored material, all clean and sweet-smelling—Grandmother's rags were always carefully washed before they were put away—pieces of chintz, of gingham, of dimity. I recognized, as was always the way in her quilts, the remains of a dress that had belonged to one of my sisters, of a blouse of Maman's, of one of my own dresses and of an apron whose owner I could no longer remember. It was pleasant to be able to attach so many memories to these scraps. Finally Grandmother found a piece of white cloth. She cut this into several bits, from which she made what looked like a number of little bags of different shapes, one for the trunk, others for arms and legs.

"Now I'll need some straw or salt or oats to stuff these with. It's up to you. Which would you prefer," she asked, "a soft doll stuffed with straw or—?"

"Oats," I said.

"It will be heavy," Grandmother warned.

"That won't matter."

"Very well then, go to the barn. There's a sack of oats there left over from the time when I was thinking of keeping some hens. Fetch me a little dishful."

When I came back, the various parts of the doll's body were all ready to be filled with the oats Mémère had saved on the chance she might have some hens. I didn't fail to notice the way a number of odd combinations of events were all rushing today to serve my pleasure. Soon my grandmother had stitched the stuffed limbs and body together and there before my eyes was a little human form, quite nicely made, with feet, hands, and a head that was a trifle flat on top.

I began to take a keen interest in the manufacture.

"But you'll be stumped for hair," I said.

"For hair? That's what you think," she said, enlivened by the discovery that the infinite and ingenious resources of her imagination, at least, were all intact. Imagination, you might say, was our family gift.

"Go back to the attic," she said. "Open the right-hand drawer of the old chest I put up there. No rummaging, mind. Just take a skein of yarn . . . By the way, do you want one of those blonde dolls that are all the rage these days? Or a brunette? Or how about an old woman with white hair like me?"

I hesitated over the cruel choice. I felt a strong inclination toward an elderly doll with spectacles and white hair, thinking what a novel effect this would present. But I also greatly fancied a young lady doll.

"Could you make me one with blond curly hair?"

"Nothing simpler," said Grandmother. "Bring the color of yarn that suits you and, on your way back, fetch my curling-iron from my room. Bring the oil lamp at the same time. No, on second thought, so you won't break something, do it in two trips."

This I proceeded to do. Grandmother then made a lovely wig of yellow hair, waved it with her curling-iron, and fitted it over my doll's head.

I could no longer hide my astonishment.

"Do you know how to make everything?" I asked.

"Almost everything," she said dreamily. "Young people nowadays don't know the joy and pride of making do with what they have at hand. They toss everything out."

And after a moment she went on, "When I was young, I had to get along without buying things in stores. I learned. Oh yes, I learned," she said, gazing far back into her life. . . . "But now your doll—she must have a face. Climb onto the table and see if you can stretch way up and snatch my pen and bottle of ink from the ledge."

When I had brought her these things, she moistened her pen and drew on the still blank face of my doll the arcs of the eyebrows first, then eyes, mouth, and a completely straight, precise little nose.

I began to clap my hands and to prance about with a joy I found it impossible to contain. No doubt it was the creative talent of my grandmother that delighted me so. Indeed, whenever I have seen this gift of God at work, even if it is possessed by the humblest creature—and it is to be found in astonishing places—it has always filled me with the keenest pleasure.

"Oh but her mouth should be red," I said.

"That's so," said Grandmother. "That blue mouth gives her a peaked look. This may present a bit of a problem. But we'll manage."

I noticed that she was beginning to associate me with her creative work and I felt prouder than ever of her talents.

"Go and look on the bureau in my room," she said with a flash of inspiration. "See if there isn't a tube of that stuff they call lipstick—atrocious stuff, real Indian war paint, but for once it will be of some use to us. It seems to me that Gertrude—no, I mean Anne-Marie—left some here the last time she went into my room to titivate."

I found just so, in the exact spot she had indicated, the Indian war paint.

With this, Grandmother drew the prettiest little red mouth, pursed just a trifle as if in a vague smile.

Curly-haired, a blond with blue eyes, my doll seemed to me now, with her rather mocking smile, to be completely beautiful, though she was still stark naked.

"To dress her," said Grandmother, "I have some very nice curtain lace in the bottom drawer of the bureau in the guest room. Go and fetch it and, while you're at it, look in the top drawer too. I think you'll find some blue ribbon there."

Half an hour later, my doll was wearing a pretty white dress, trimmed with ruffles and a sky-blue sash, and Grandmother was busily stitching a row of minute blue buttons down the front of the dress.

"But she's barefoot," I said suddenly in consternation. "Shoes will be a little harder, eh, Mémère?"

I was becoming humble, very humble indeed before her, before the grandeur of her mind, the deftness of her hands, the sense of exalted and mysterious solitude that surrounds all those who are busy with creation.

"Shoes," she said simply. "Would you like them made of leather or satin or plush?"

"Oh, of leather!"

"Yes, it's more durable. Well then, go and fetch the yellow leather gloves that used to belong to your uncle Nicolas. You will find them . . ."

This time too, under her directions, I put my hand without trouble on the yellow leather gloves.

"It's store leather," she said, turning them about and peering at them closely. "Stores sell mostly rubbish, badly stitched, badly finished. For once something handsome and of good quality has come from one of those places. Your uncle Nicolas had extravagant tastes in his youth," she confided. "But it's true that he bought these gloves for his wedding. Now you see how everything can be of service more than once. Yesterday for a wedding, today for dolls' shoes. They say I keep everything, that I encumber myself, that I'm an old-fashioned old woman. But a day always comes when the things you tossed out of the window might have been put to good use."

While she was talking, she first cut out, then put together the most adorable little dolls' shoes I had ever seen.

"While I'm at it," she said, "I might as well make her some gloves."

Night came. Grandmother had me light the lamp and bring it close to her. Neither of us thought of the evening meal. The strict daily schedule to which my grandmother held so firmly for once had ceased to exist. So when something bigger than the timetable presented itself, she was quite able to ignore it. She went on working, her glasses on her nose, as happy, I am convinced, as in the days when urgent tasks claimed her from morning till night, leaving her, you might say, no moment's respite in which to scrutinize the vast enigmatic depths of fate. Or perhaps I should say happy with a completeness she knew only when her task transcended the bare requirements of the moment.

"Have you thought of a name for her?" she asked, looking at me from under her spectacles.

They were old spectacles with steel rims.

"Yes. Anastasie."

"Ah!" she said, and I knew that the name pleased her. "There was an Anastasie in my village in Quebec in the old days. It's a striking name, not like these little short modern names that you forget the very next minute: Jean, Jeanne, Robert, Roberte. . . . In the old days people had names you could remember—Phidime, Viateur, Zoé, Sosthène, Zacharie. . . ."

All this time my doll was progressing. She didn't, it might be said, need anything else, but Grandmother was undoubtedly too well launched by now to be able to stop. From some black cloth she fashioned a traveling cape, then—one thing suggesting another—painstakingly set to work with cardboard and glue to make her a little valise. To this she stitched a minute handle, which I slipped over Anastasie's hand.

Even this wasn't enough.

"She must have a hat," Grandmother declared. "One doesn't go traveling without a hat, even in these shameless modern times."

She sent me to fetch an old straw hat from behind the door of the vestibule. She unraveled it, then, working slowly with her rheumatism-stiffened fingers—with such fingers, she told me, it was much more difficult to work with small things than with large—she knitted a new, this time tiny, dainty hat.

"What!" I cried, quite overcome. "So you know how to make hats too!"

"In the old days I made very pretty hats from the fine marsh straw not far from our house. . . . Not only that," she told me, "I have often dressed someone—your mother, your grandfather—from head to foot. . . ."

"From head to foot, Mémère!"

"From head to foot . . . and without needing to go to the store for a single thing, except perhaps for buttons . . . And I've even made those out of ox horn; with an awl to pierce the holes, I managed."

"From head to foot!" I said.

She held out my doll with her straw hat hanging from her neck by a ribbon. I was so happy that I burst into tears.

"Well, if we're going to have that again, if I've done all this for nothing!" Grandmother said in grumbling tones.

But, forgetting how little she cared for effusiveness or caresses, I climbed onto her knees, flung my arms around her neck, and sobbed with a happiness that was too piercing and wide to bear, almost incredible. It seemed to me that there was no limit to the things this old woman with the face covered with a thousand wrinkles could accomplish. A sense of grandeur, of infinite solitude, came over me.

"You're like God," I wept into her ear. "You're just like God. You can make things out of nothing as he does."

She pushed me away but without too much exasperation or impatience.

"I'm far from being like God," she said. "Do you think I'd know how to make a tree, a flower, a mountain?"

"A flower, perhaps."

She smiled a little. "I've certainly made plenty of them grow."

Nevertheless, I saw that she wasn't offended by my comparing her to God.

"For with such means and strength as he gave me," she said after a moment's reflection, "I have aided him not too badly in his creation. I have perhaps done all a human being could do. I have twice built a home," she told me, "having followed your trotting horse of a grandfather from one part of this vast country to another. I began all over again here in Manitoba what I'd already made back in Quebec, made once for all, I thought—a home. That is work," she assured me. "Yes—a house, a family—that's so much work that if you saw it before you all at once in a single heap, you'd think it was a high mountain—a mountain you couldn't possibly climb over."

She realized that I was listening to her, Anastasie clutched against my heart, but perhaps thought it all passed over me —and indeed most of it did, though I kept a little of it.

"That is what life is, if you want to know," she continued, and I no longer knew to whom she was speaking, "a mountain made of housework. It's a good thing you don't see it at the outset; if you did you mightn't risk it, you'd balk. But the mountain only shows itself as you climb it. Not only that, no matter how much housework you do in your life, just as much remains for those who come after you. Life is work that's never finished. And in spite of that, when you're shoved into a corner to rest, not knowing what to do with your ten fingers, do you know what happens?" she asked, and, without waiting for an answer, told me, "Well, you're bored to death; you may even miss the housework. Can you make anything out of that?"

"No," I said.

She seemed utterly astonished to discover me, all attention, at her feet.

"Are you mad at someone?" I asked.

"Mind your own business," she said.

But an instant later, withdrawn again into her reveries, she named for me, one by one, all those who had so bitterly offended her.

"Your grandfather Elisée . . . such a trick to play on me,

the gay adventurer . . . to go first, without waiting for me, leaving me all alone on this western prairie, in exile."

"Manitoba isn't exile," I said. "It's home."

"All the rest of you too," she went on. "You'll be just like the others. You're all like him—independent, selfish, travelers every one of you. You all have to be off somewhere. . . . And God too—even he in many ways has forsaken me. Because truly, no matter what the priests say, no matter how hard they try to make reason and sense out of it, he allows too many strange worrisome things to happen to us."

She grumbled on so that I dozed, leaning against her knees, my doll in my arms, and saw my grandmother storm into Paradise with a great many things to complain about. In my dream God the Father, with his great beard and stern expression, yielded his place to Grandmother, with her keen, shrewd, far-seeing eyes. From now on it would be she, seated in the clouds, who would take care of the world, set up wise and just laws. Now all would be well for the poor people on earth.

For a long time I was haunted by the idea that it could not possibly be a man who made the world. But perhaps an old woman with extremely capable hands.

2

Yet a year or so later my grandmother, powerful as she seemed to me, began to be a source of constant worry to my mother.

"Foolhardy as she is," said Maman, "I just can't rest knowing she's alone in that little solitary house. She might fall while pulling up that trapdoor leading to her cellar and lie there heaven knows how long with a broken hip before anyone noticed they hadn't seen her go out."

I was astonished by this perpetual anxiety, for to me, I suppose, Grandmother seemed indestructible.

One day it was a presentiment Maman had had, another day a dream in which she had seen Grandmother calling to her from the bottom of a well.

Finally, one such morning, Maman got up firmly decided to go that very day to bring her mother back to live with us. I was already rejoicing, thinking of the lovely dressmaking I would see as soon as Grandmother was at our house.

But Maman returned unsuccessful.

"Just imagine what I found her doing," she said as soon as she came in, still wearing her hat but already seated to tell us about her disappointment, so that she still seemed to be a visitor in her own house. "When I think of it! At this time of year, when the soil is still damp and cold, there she was in her field—her prairie as she calls it—digging."

I for my part didn't find this so terrible. Every year at this season, it was an undeniable fact that Grandmother was to be seen turning the soil, and I supposed that this was because she liked to do it.

"Yes, indeed," said Maman, as if infuriated by the very thought, "this year again she's undertaken a huge garden. 'Really, Maman,' I asked her, 'do you consider it sensible for one solitary old woman to grow enough vegetables to feed a whole township?'"

To this Grandmother had replied, as seemed to me quite in character, "You may be happy to have some of my vegetables yourself," then something else like, "It's my own business . . ." which Maman reported to us in Grandmother's voice,

slipping back into her own as she said, "I think it's my
business too. . . ."

In this way one could follow everything that had happened
quite well, Maman having a talent for recounting animated
discussions between two or three people.

"Just stop making yourself so anxious about me," Maman
told us her mother had said, to which she herself had replied, "Ah, now I don't have to make myself anxious!"

I was so fond of such accounts in those days that I believe
I was too interested to realize how sad it essentially was.

"She has aged so incredibly," said Maman. "I watched her
coming and going and I became aware of it all at once.
It's curious. Apparently we don't notice from day to day or
from year to year that our parents are growing old. Then
suddenly we find ourselves before the irreparable."

Then, because her mother had grown old, Maman herself looked a great deal older and began to cry.

It was strange, though. In order to make us see how old
her mother had become, Maman needed first, it seemed, to
make us see her as she'd been when she was young.

"You know that she was considered a very beautiful woman
in her time?"

No, we hadn't known.

"With sparkling eyes and abundant jet-black hair. And
such a carriage! And her memory too: just like her drawers,
beautifully tidy, in perfect order, dates, names, every event
in its place. She was a remarkable person," said Maman.

"And now?" I asked, thinking chiefly of the drawers.

"Let me give you an example," said Maman. "Twice in
the same day she asked me what year I was born and how old
that made me."

I did not find this so shocking, doubtless because Grandmother had so often had to ask me too, "How old are you?"

Even my name, which I must admit had disconcerted me a little. The thing that confounded me most was Maman herself, the way her face changed, becoming sad and tender when she spoke of Grandmother when she was young, then only sad and despondent. I could make almost nothing more of this coming and going of one human being through the memory of another. A grandmother who was old and who might perhaps grow a little older I could admit, but a grandmother with a brisk step, fiery eyes, and thick black hair I could not. I suppose I must have believed that Grandmother had always been old.

Maman had come to the moment in her story when she had been obliged to part from Grandmother, reluctant to leave her alone but not knowing what else she could do. As stubborn as ever, her mother declared that she wasn't ready yet to give up her own concerns, her independence. It was as if she believed herself assured of ten years of life still to come. Or perhaps she knew this wasn't so and simply wished to make use of whatever time might remain to her in her own way.

"And I?" Maman asked us. "Can I be in two places at once, here where I'm needed and there where I may be needed quite as much?"

"No," we told Maman to console her, "no one can be in two places at once."

She thanked us with a smile. The thing that kept gnawing at her, she admitted, was the sense that she had been close to victory over Mémère.

"I was on the doorstep, you understand. I was slipping on my gloves. It was a gray lifeless morning. You know what the countryside is like there in early spring—almost as bare as in the fall. You can scarcely believe it will ever come to life again. I could have sworn at that moment that if I could just have found the right word . . . The ax quivered, I do believe. . . . But then a flock of migrating birds passed across the sky, and your grandmother lifted her head. That was the chief thing I had to contend with, that wretched springtime, the little seeds she'd entrusted to the earth, her savory, her petunias that were just about to come up, she said. Even so, she felt a certain fear at seeing me go.

" 'You'll come back soon?' she asked.

" 'Yes, Maman, but you mustn't be stubborn for too long. One of these days you'll have to come.'

" 'We'll see. . . . We'll see . . .' she said, doing her best to hide her vertigo and dizziness. From the threshold she looked ahead of her at the naked prairie about which she has complained so bitterly all her life, saying that it wearied her to death, that she would never get used to it, that it would never be her country . . . and yet I wonder if it isn't that same prairie that holds her there so strongly today—her old enemy, or what she believed was her enemy. . . ."

3

From my point of view it seemed that the very next day it was the lovely autumn. It didn't sadden me at that time. The days were short, and often somber, but we kept a good fire going in the house, we ate pumpkin pie, we sorted walnuts and corn. We also set tomatoes to ripen on the window sills, and on certain days the whole house was permeated with the odor of pickles cooking over a gentle fire in large pans. The saw could be heard singing in the yard; its two-toned song, first clear, then deeper and heavier as it bit into the wood, seemed to me to promise us joyfully, "I'm cutting you fine logs, fine logs for the whole winter." All this time the house, like a ship ready to weigh anchor or a city about to undergo a siege, was being filled with provisions—sauerkraut, maple syrup from Quebec, red apples from British Columbia, plums from Ontario. Soon also we began to receive from our uncles in the country fat geese and turkeys, dozens of chickens, hams and salt bacon, cases of fresh eggs and farm butter. To help ourselves, we had only to go into our summer kitchen, now transformed into a storehouse, where the frost preserved our stock. Such were the joys of autumn, based upon abundance and a feeling of security that I think I appreciated even then. But Maman, who had also always greatly loved the autumn, this year, as she devoted herself to the occupations it demanded, seemed to do so grudgingly. She gathered things in, it might be said, without joy and even with a sort of sorrow, all the time close in spirit to her mother. "She too," she said, "will have brought in her cucumbers and squash. She too will have preserved as much as possible. But for what purpose? Poor old woman, what will be the use to her of all that work?" And the idea grazed me lightly that it must indeed be heartbreaking to have one's cupboards full, one's pantry stuffed to the bursting point, one's cellar perfumed with great cabbages, gooseberry jam on the shelves, things to eat everywhere, and no longer anyone to offer them to.

The days grew even shorter, and this was increasingly to my taste. Like all the children in that part of the world, I longed for snow. I dreamed that it had come down during my sleep in swift flakes, preparing that beautiful pure-white world that I believed I loved best, though when it melted with the coming of spring into a thousand restless little streams, this too I believed I loved above everything else.

One morning Maman, who had also always loved the winter, as she loved the other seasons, began to lament as she looked out the slightly frosted window, "Winter already! How sad that is!"

And she set out before the day was over to go, as she put it, to give yet one more shake to the tree.

Two days later the weather was bad, wonderfully bad, I should say, for I loved to see the snow puff up and rise and wander high in the sky in ceaselessly changing shapes that might even be half alive, for I believed I could hear them shouting with happiness at being finally set free by the storm. Then, as I stood at the window, fascinated by this dance of the snow, I saw at the end of the street a rather old woman helping another who was much older down from a streetcar, both of them somberly dressed, the younger of the two carrying a suitcase and an ancient umbrella. I shall never be able to forget how black the figures of my mother and her mother looked that evening against the uniform whiteness of the landscape.

The moment she had helped her mother take off her "bonnet" and "cloak"—right till the end Grandmother continued to have a different vocabulary from ours—Maman led her to a big old chair that she had upholstered and forbidden us to sit in even before Mémère arrived at our house.

"That will be her chair," she would say. "At least leave her her chair."

Grandmother, however, did not seem as pleased as Maman had hoped.

"Do you think I want to spend my life sitting down now?" she asked.

"Why no," said Maman. "You will come and go. You will make yourself perfectly at home."

"At home!" Grandmother replied, looking about her with displeasure. "Don't fancy that I'm going to drag on here forever."

The thing that astonished us most from this day on was Maman's attitude. After having stood up to her mother till that time, she now almost always agreed with her.

"You will stay only as long as you wish, Maman."

But she told us privately that while Grandmother was packing her suitcase she had, quite casually, slipped her "booty" into the bottom.

By her "booty" Grandmother meant her finest underwear and bed linen, which she had been working at for a good part of her life and which she was saving, she always said, for "a time to come." What time could this be? And why did Grandmother put off using her "booty" till so late? But, it is true, the old women of those days did nothing as we do today.

Winter was so delightful to me at that time and I had so much to do—building forts or making hills of snow and sliding down them on my sleigh, a pastime I was able to continue almost till nightfall, for I had a lantern made of a candle in an old jam tin with a slit in it attached to the front of my sleigh to light my way—so much to do that I scarcely noticed what was happening to Grandmother from one day to the next. I would come in, my cheeks reddened from the cold, my eyes sparkling, excited by my games, and I would see, huddled at the end of the kitchen, an aged person whose eyes followed all our comings and goings with a strange expression. I couldn't rid myself of the notion that it was not my real grandmother Maman had brought to our house that snowy evening. She must have made a mistake and brought someone else. For my real grandmother would never have been able to remain idle. She had always said it would kill her to sit about with nothing to do.

But one day she grew angry and demanded some work. "Some work," said Maman. "Haven't you done enough in your life?"

But just the same she gave her a few towels to hem.

And the old, old woman who lived among us in her corner began to examine the fabric, testing its resistance by pulling it from all sides, only to declare at last that it was far from being as good as that she had woven in her time.

She was continually feeling material now, the material of our clothes and curtains and household linen. She made fun of it, saying it was nothing but trash. To hear her speak, everything in our house was cheap, store-bought trash. Sometimes, at certain words, I pricked up my ears, believing that I had recognized for a moment the voice of my grandmother.

But immediately afterward there would be only a mumble and I would return to my idea of the substitution of persons.

The towels made scarcely any progress, and the old person in our house got it into her head that she would rather knit some heavy black stockings, of a sort, moreover, that almost no one wore any more. When she reached the heel, the whole thing became muddled up and she scolded away about the wool of today that didn't knit up well. Maman in secret partly unraveled the stocking and redid it to the place where her mother had stopped. Grandmother noticed just the same and complained that the goblins must have tangled her wool during the night. I was astonished by this, having myself stopped believing in goblins a long time before. Maman explained that this was a belief from the time of Grandmother's childhood and that such beliefs had a tendency to be reborn in extreme old age.

No doubt it was this that muddled me up in my turn: that in Grandmother's case one spoke at once of old age and of second childhood. I was still not more than half persuaded that it was really she who lived with us, but I began to study her from closer at hand. At that time scarcely anything remained to her but speech, if speech it could be called. Maman claimed, however, that we did not make enough effort to listen to Grandmother and that later we might be sorry we hadn't gathered in the last confidences of a life, that these were a sort of inestimable treasure that was offered only rarely in the course of an existence.

One day when they believed themselves alone together, I listened to them sharing this treasure, and all I heard was this:

Maman: "When one reaches your age, Maman, what does life seem to be?"

Grandmother: "A dream, my daughter, not much more than a dream."

Another day, when Maman had interrupted her work to go to sit beside Grandmother and try to make out what she was saying by following the movement of her lips, she flung us a look at once melancholy and triumphant.

"Do you know what she's just said to me?" (For it was as if Grandmother needed her now to interpret her words to us, and no one was better in this role than Maman.) "She said, 'Eveline, do you remember the little Assomption River?'"

The Assomption River! What river was this of which I was hearing for the first time in my life?

"It's a little river in the hills where she was born," Maman explained. "I didn't know she had thought of it so much. But do try to understand. The Assomption River is a little of your Grandmother's youth, far away, in Quebec."

What was there to understand? The Assomption River I
could manage to picture a little: a pretty and capricious
river, I was told, that flowed swiftly at times, then suddenly
took its own time to idle into coves. But those other things
—the frank speech, the courage, the piercing sight—where
were all these things that had once belonged to Grandmother,
as Maman said, and how could she have let them be lost?

I played with less spirit now. Often I came back to the
house for nothing, simply to see what was happening and to
give a glance at the aged person who was "losing" more all
the time.

We had got into the way, I don't know how, of speaking of
her while she was present. Maman begged us to be careful.

"Perhaps she still hears us. Her look follows us, in any
event, and perhaps she's accusing us."

One evening when Maman was helping her into bed, her
mother seized her by the hand, drew her close, and lamented
into her ear, "Not good for anything any more . . . just a
nuisance . . . want to go away . . ."

"You want to go away? Certainly, Maman, some day very
soon we'll go away. We'll all go."

Was this really my grandmother whom one day in my
childish naïveté I had believed to be like God, or one of his
best helpers at least, occupied every day of her busy life pro-
viding on earth for human needs? I was beginning to
understand that no one was almighty except him, but then
why did he need, as Maman said, to reduce us sometimes to
total impotence? My hard-working grandmother lay paralyzed
from head to foot, only her eyes still alive. At least Maman
insisted that they were.

"I'm sure she's still conscious," she said. "Poor soul, we
must try to reach her again."

She was the only one who discovered the way. She would

stay close to this immobile block under the covers that she continued to call Maman, and I cannot describe the derangement I experienced at hearing my mother, old as she seemed to me at that time, speaking with this child's word to someone who could no longer eat or drink alone. I felt such an unutterable confusion about ages, about childhood and old age, that it seemed to me I would never get myself out of it. It was rather as if Maman were taking care of a baby. But does one ask a baby, does one say to it, "Your conscience is clear, isn't it? You've always done your duty. Why should you fear?"?

From time to time she would become aware of me, always at her skirts, as if her task were not complicated enough without that, and she would try to send me away, but gently, "Go outside. Go and play." And I would see her eyes fill with pity, for me as well as for Mémère, for everyone perhaps, as if Maman had taken everyone in the world into her pity, and to me also at that time everyone must have seemed in need of pity.

She seldom succeeded in sending me away. I was drawn, far more than by my usual games, by this other sort of game in which my mother seemed to be engaged, seated near her own mother and interrogating her—a strange game of questions to which there were very seldom answers—"Won't you eat a little? Some good chicken broth I've made especially for you?"

At times the eyes closed. I myself believed it was in weariness from all these questions. But according to Maman it meant "Yes," and she would hurry, pleased, she said, at still being able to do something for one who had done so much for her.

Most often, though, the eyes remained fixed. And so far from us. Maman would be grief-stricken.

"Yet there must be something that she wishes. But what?"

"Something that she wishes," I said to myself in my turn. What could someone wish for who had nothing more to lose but her eyes? To look at something, probably. But what? One day when I was passing the room in which Grandmother lay, quite alone for the moment, I went in timidly. At first I kept far from the bed, looking elsewhere, at the beautiful lace curtains, for instance, that Maman had recently and at long last taken from her drawers. They were thrifty women, she and Grandmother; they put off using their "booty," it seemed to me, until too late. Finally I risked a glance from the side of Grandmother's bed. I met her eyes. They were of a living brown, still beautiful, and they seemed to be asking me to come closer. I think it was at this moment that I finally surrendered to the truth that this was my grandmother. I drew closer. I whispered, as if I still weren't entirely sure, or because I was a little bit afraid, "Mémère."

I thought of asking, as Maman did, "Are you hungry? Are you thirsty?" But it soon occurred to me that Mémère couldn't care very much for this and that her wishes, if she still had any, must be for something quite different.

It may have been because Maman, at the time when her mother was resisting her, had spoken so often of going to give a shake to the tree, but Grandmother at this moment really made me think of a poor old oak, isolated from the others, alone on a little hill. Perhaps this was the source of another curious idea, which has remained with me, that trees also have a grievance in a sense, enclosed in their tough bark, their feet held fast in the earth, unable to go away if they wish. Though who can come and go as he desires? I dreamed, seated in my turn beside Grandmother, dreamed about trees, I think. Then an odd picture came to me. I seemed to see, lower down, some young trees, which were perhaps born of the old tree on the hillside but, still decked in all their leaves, sang in the valley. It was this image, I believe, that gave me a most brilliant idea. I ran down to the living room to fetch the photograph album. It was a big bulky book, bound in green velvet, with gold clasps. I went up again, the book pressed against my chest. I sat down beside the bed. I turned the pages.

On almost every one of them I came upon someone who was, as the expression goes, descended from Mémère. I went over and held the book before her eyes.

"You have lots of folks of your own, eh?" I said. "Look, Mémère."

Then, remembering that when I had visited her two years before, she had already had difficulty finding her way among her grandchildren, I began to call off their names, coupling each one, when I could, with a face in the album. In this way, it seemed to me, Grandmother would be able to gather once more into her mind all those who belonged to her.

It was a fine pastime and I set myself to it with ardor. I hoped to forget no one and, especially, to reach a hundred, a figure I respected enormously at that time. But would I reach it? Perhaps, if I counted the dead . . . But had one the right to, in a list such as I was making? It seemed to me that one hadn't. I didn't know what death was. To my mind it was a simple matter of disappearance. One day people were there . . . another day, they were not. . . . Besides, among the dead people in the album, there were some I hadn't even known. Was it worth mentioning them? And yet the more names I had to offer Mémère, it seemed to me, the more enclosed she would feel. And so it came about that, as I turned the pages, I found her there herself, still young, seated beside her husband, among her children, some of them standing behind her, the younger ones on the grass at her feet. This old photograph fascinated me so much that

I forgot everything else. Through it, at last, I think I began to understand vaguely a little about life and all the successive beings it makes of us as we increase in age. I raised my eyes from the album and compared the photograph with the original. There was not much resemblance. I came, with the book open at that page, to show my grandmother the portrait she no longer resembled.

"You were beautiful in those days," I said.

Did her eyes not sparkle a little? Perhaps . . . But at that moment I noticed Maman in the doorway. She had come up without a sound and must have been standing there motionless for a moment, watching and listening to me. She gave me a sad and very tender little smile.

But why did she look so pleased with me? I was only playing, as she herself had taught me to do, as Mémère also had played with me one day . . . as we all play perhaps, throughout our lives, at trying to catch up with one another.

The Old Man and the Child

I WAS unhappy for a long time about the death of my grandmother. Then came a strange summer and, as if as a consolation, I made the acquaintance of a sweet and marvelous old man.

He lived not far from us on a gently sloping little street where I used to like to go with my roller skates or my hoop. Everything moved more quickly there than elsewhere, my skates, my hoop, I myself, and the wind in my ears. This distracted me.

And yet no one but me had discovered that this street went downward, flowed a trifle; even when I insisted, they didn't believe me.

But the day I met the old man I wasn't going quickly. On the contrary, I was advancing painfully, mounted on my stilts. Where did the children in our part of the world at that time get their fondness for perching up high? (Our land was flat as the palm of the hand, dry and without obstacles.) Was it to see far across the level prairie? Or even farther still, into the future?

So I was struggling with difficulty along the hot, silent little street, which was so somnolent one would have thought there was nothing alive on it but the old man who always sat on a straight chair in the middle of a bit of skimpy grass, in the shade of a young maple—the only tree planted on that street, so that it too was better known to us than any other tree in our town.

The old man saw me from far away, very visible on my stilts, and at once he seemed to come to life to follow my progress, assisting me with his pleasant little light-blue eyes, holding me up at every step, obviously anxious on my behalf.

I came closer.

And then, as happens so often in life when one is too anxious to excel and win the approval of an attentive and benevolent spectator, I missed a step and sprawled full length upon the pavement.

Such consternation as I saw on the face of the old man! He ran toward me. He helped me to get up and shake the dust from my dress; he examined the wound on my knee, showing concern but not too much. It was courage he valued. As soon as he had made sure I wasn't badly hurt, he began to praise my efforts.

"Walking on stilts isn't a thing everyone would try. It requires agility and nerve. You have to be young too."

"When you were little," I asked—and that seemed to me a thousand years ago—"did you ever try?"

"No," he said, "but I pretended to limp and to need crutches."

This made me see in him a rare companion. On certain days I had walked for a fair distance purposely limping. From then on, it seemed to me, we would be able to speak freely and intimately about almost everything.

"It's hot," I said, wiping the sweat from my forehead.

"Very hot," he said, "especially for one who is making a journey."

So he already knew that I was on a journey, far away, in a foreign country.

"Good-by," I said. "I must catch up with the others."

He pulled out his watch and consulted it, then made a little dry sound with his tongue against the roof of his mouth, his features meanwhile expressing alarmed astonishment.

"Why, that's true," he said. "It's late. You have just enough time, just enough time."

First thing next morning, I ran in great haste to the little street. As soon as I turned the corner, I saw the old man already seated in the shade of the maple. I leaned over the fence.

"We're early birds," I said.

"Yes, we are. You have to be when you're old or when you're young. It's the people between who stay longest in bed. The rest of us, the very old and the very young, haven't time for that, eh?"

"No, we haven't."

"You're on foot today?"

"Yes. Because I'm going a long way."

He didn't seem in the least astonished by this logic.

"Who are you today?" he asked.

So he already knew that I was not often merely myself. At the instant someone spoke to me, I might be the Chinese laundryman going about collecting the dirty clothes, or the old Italian vegetable seller, in which case, however, I usually made myself known by shouting on all sides, with what I believed to be an Italian accent, "Banania, banania." I might also be a princess. But today I was someone so remarkable, such a personage, that I could no longer keep from exclaiming, "La Vérendrye! I'm La Vérendrye!"

"Oh my! La Vérendrye. Isn't that something! My, my. The greatest explorer in Canada. If I remember well, he hasn't been seen around these parts for at least a hundred years."

"More than a hundred years. And I must go and discover all the territories of the west right up to the Rocky Mountains," I said. "If I'm not killed on the way, I shall have taken possession of the west before evening for the King of France."

"Oh isn't that a good idea," said the old man approvingly, "to go first, before the English, and gather those territories under our flag. Have a good journey," he said.

I made my farewell.

Then he asked, "If you are successful, if the enterprise goes well, will you pass this way again?"

"Yes, monsieur," I said, "I will pass this very same way and make you a report." (This expression, which I had got from my father, I loved to such an extent that everything with me was an excuse for a report.)

"For, you see, Monsieur La Vérendrye," said the old man, "I myself am past the age for long exhausting journeys. I am not likely to go again in person to contemplate the landscapes and spectacles of this world. But if you come and describe them to me, it will be as if I were there once more."

"I will come."

"Without fail?"

"Without fail."

And I hurried as quickly as I could toward the little grove of oaks at the foot of the short street, where a sort of open countryside began.

In the little grove of oaks I searched for acorns, making a show of doing something; I was actually only there to let a few minutes pass by, to allow time at least for my explorations to be carried out. As for the account I would have to give, I wasn't in the least troubled; for that I trusted to improvisation. But suddenly, as I sat in the midst of these somber little trees, a sense of lassitude came over me and I no longer knew what I had come there to find or why. It is true that often that summer I was visited in the midst of my games by the memory of my grandmother as I had seen her lying in her coffin, her face hard as rock, surrounded by people who prayed in voices whose accent tore my heart. I don't know what fugitive and swift misgivings crossed my mind in these moments, clarifying nothing, revealing nothing, and yet leaving me each time more anxious. I daresay I had not yet clearly understood that we shall all end thus, that this will be our final image of those we love best, but I had at least an inkling that old wrinkled faces were closer to this than I was myself. Then was it this, a sort of prescience I had of their approaching disappearance, that made them so dear to me? But then, why were they, the old people, similarly drawn to me? Was it not because it is natural that small, scarcely formed hands and old whittled-down hands should come together? But there again, who can explain a phenomenon that is itself as full of mystery as that of life, or of death in a coffin?

After ten or fifteen minutes I returned from the Rockies. I appeared again at the fence.

"I've seen them," I announced with shining eyes, as if, on the rim of our monotonous horizon of Manitoba, flat and level as it is, I had suddenly come upon their astonishing dreamy masses.

The old man roused from a light doze. His eyes sparkled, as lively as a fire that catches well.

"Is it possible? So you went so far? You've actually seen the Rockies? Ah, tell me about it."

I told him about it, about the mountains that were higher even than telephone poles, about the hordes of bison I had come across along the way, and also how I had suffered for days and days from hunger and thirst.

"That doesn't surprise me," said the old man. "To have undertaken such a dangerous expedition! Did you at least take the necessary precautions? And is it as hot there?"

"Even worse, if possible. On the tenth day of the journey I found heaps of dry bones on the plain. Animals and people are dead. Everyone is suffocating, and there is naught but dust in the sun." (I had got this from one of my books. *"Sister Anne, what do you see?"* . . . *"I see naught but dust in the sun and the green grass growing by the road."*)

And then I asked, "What does that mean—naught but dust?" and the old man explained it to me.

2

Everyone was saying at that time that never, never in the memory of man, had Manitoba experienced a hotter and more distressing summer. But it seems to me that all through my childhood years I heard exactly the same thing said of every summer. Poor people; scarcely had we left the brutal winter behind than we entered a sort of forge, which baked us as if to teach us what came of daring to complain while it was cold. Ah, so you froze, you were chilled to the bone? said the summer. Well, now learn what it is to be hot.

My dear old friend, spare and thin as he was, may not have suffered from the heat as much as fat people did, but he did suffer and, sitting under his tree, he tried to make a little breeze for himself by shaking his folded newspaper before his face.

However, merely to go to sit under his tree—or a little farther, to take a few steps along the street—he was always neat and clean, as if he were holding himself in readiness for the important visit, which, he had told me, might take place at any moment. That he, who was always so alone on this silent street, might have a visitor at last was surprising enough in itself. Nevertheless, the old man confided to me, although he had been expecting this visit for a long time and kept himself ready and neat for it, nevertheless it would almost certainly take him by surprise.

So, whether he was under his tree or elsewhere, I never saw him untidy, but always completely buttoned up, with his tie knotted and wearing a jacket of a sort of black linen, his old hands with their swollen veins pinching the creases of his trousers from time to time. Traces of a wide-toothed comb could be seen in his white beard. He must also have liked to keep his ears clean, for I remember a frequent little gesture of his: he would insert the tip of his little finger, then shake it as if to dislodge the wax. In addition, from morning till night he wore a very elegant white straw hat with a black ribbon, which he had bought, he told me, in the Caribbees.

One evening when the air, according to my mother, had freshened slightly, we saw the old man coming along our street, just as I have described him except that he had his cane. He was walking with slow steps, but with his body erect and his head held high, as if the dew, which had revived the flowers in our garden that evening, had rejuvenated him also a little.

"Why, it's Monsieur Saint-Hilaire," Maman exclaimed. And she asked, "How are you, Monsieur Saint-Hilaire?"

For the first time I realized that he was slightly deaf, for with a pleasant smile he replied, "Yes, a refreshing little breeze."

"And your children?" Maman inquired. "Are they well?" This time the old man understood.

"Yes, very well," he said.

At least they had been well according to the last news he'd had of them, which wasn't very recent.

During this exchange of words I had been acting as if I no longer quite recognized my old friend. Why did I do this, perhaps causing pain to the old man, who was screwing up his eyes, undoubtedly trying to make me out from among the group seated on the gallery, having perhaps come as far as our house only to find me? I daresay it was out of some sort of jealousy and perhaps also from a wish to keep the secrecy and mystery of our understanding intact. But one thing was certain: I already detested these sons and daughters-in-law of whom my mother was speaking No doubt I had imagined that the old man had no one in the world but me and that I was everything to him.

When he had gone a little distance from us, Maman sighed. "Poor Monsieur Saint-Hilaire," she said. "Here he is, after bringing up a family, almost all alone in the world."

I learned that evening that he could not live with his daughter, whom he had spoiled and cherished, on account of her husband, with whom he had squabbled, nor with his son because he had fallen out with the latter's wife. So he had had to go and board with strangers.

"Perhaps the best thing under the circumstances," Maman

acknowledged, "since the poor man is still so set in his opinions and, I'm afraid, of a positive and dictatorial disposition that may not always be easy to live with."

I turned to my mother defiantly. Did she think I would accept the man she was describing as my dear old Monsieur Saint-Hilaire?

He had come from France when he was very young, she continued, letting it be understood that his being French explained to some extent his peculiar ideas and his behavior that might perhaps be hard to put up with, though it also gave him his particular interest in her eyes. He had married in Canada, she said, established a home, and made quite a nice little fortune by the manufacture of macaroni and pasta under various brand names. His children, whom he'd brought up in luxury, must have squandered most of it, but he'd managed, in his provident French way, to secure a small pension for his old age. Still, it was a long way, she concluded, from the Monsieur Saint-Hilaire of former days, lord and master in his own house, to this little old man walking all alone in thě twilight, as if he were looking for someone . . . in our street. . . .

These last words distressed me. I imagined the visitor he had expected for so long choosing the one brief instant he was away to turn up finally at his door. Because of me, perhaps, they might have missed each other. . . . But everything else Maman had said about Monsieur Saint-Hilaire I thrust away as quite incredible. It couldn't be possible that he was a difficult old man and that he had made a nice little round sum from pasta. None of these words pleased me. And, anyway, how could a sum of money be round?

Of course, with the dawn next day came the return of the blazing heat. We had to get up very early, unable to stand being in bed any longer on account of the fierce sun that already beat through the roof. Nor could we retire till the night was well advanced, since the heat took so long to disperse. So we got too little sleep and we were all more or less enervated.

How curious is this so-called cold country of ours! There were times enough certainly when we couldn't cover ourselves with sufficient wool and fur. So it seemed harder for us than for others to be longing so desperately for cold now that we must seek out the tiniest bits of shade.

As soon as she went out onto the gallery each morning, my mother would announce in a discouraged voice after the first breath of the parched air, with no need of a thermometer to support her prognostications, "Today it will go up to ninety-eight, perhaps ninety-nine."

This morning she reached one hundred, a figure I found more satisfactory than a mere ninety-nine.

She looked at me with concern.

"Ah," she said, "if only I could send you to the country."

I dreamed of it, of course. In the long run, weren't we always dreaming in Manitoba of something other than what we had—during the hard winter, of the time when the sun would glitter; and when it became implacable, of quantities of snow to refresh us? And so we lived, rather like everyone else on the face of the earth, I imagine, little satisfied with the present, in constant expectation of the future, and often in regret for what was past. But thanks be to heaven that, whatever happens, there remain always, on either side of us, those two open doors.

Perhaps, even so, the heat was less distressing to us than the drought. Everything was wilting, everything dying. A single little shower would have so much benefited our lives and our gardens. But we had had too much rain when we shouldn't have had, while the wheat was being sown; and now when water might still have saved the little that had managed to grow, none came and the sky was too calm to permit hope of any.

I went, doleful and out of sorts, to find the old man. I had no imagination for games these days. My thoughts were like the listless leaves on the trees of this motionless summer; none of them stirred or quivered. I have known this misery often enough in my life since then, and perhaps nothing has been more frankly intolerable to me; even grief crushes me less than this insensitivity—might one not say this indifference?— on our own part to our own thought.

Above the old man the maple tree was steady as a garden parasol. Undoubtedly a tree that imitates a parasol is beautiful, but even more beautiful is a tree that lives with the sun and the wind and plays incessantly at separating its leaves, as if they were hair, to see below perhaps. I watched to see whether the foliage would part into one of those lovely slits through which blue can be seen. It did not. Below, in the calm air, the old man's breathing was the only sound.

He placed his hand on my forehead, for I was sitting on the yellowed grass at his feet. It was the first little caress he had dared to give me.

"How hot you are," he said solicitously.

On his face, which was like an old piece of soil pitted and cracked by the drought, I saw a thread of sweat flowing down a single furrow, one drop of moisture for all this old dry soil.

"You are too," I said compassionately.

He looked down at me with his shrewd and kindly eyes.

"How is it that you're not in the country?" he asked me. "You look a bit dejected and skinny. You need some good milk and plenty of fresh air. Don't you know anyone in the country who would have you?"

"Oh yes," I said. "We have lots of family in the country."

"Well then?"

"Well, so!" I said, raising my arms toward the sky in that curious gesture of despair I had copied from one of my aunts, the one who was always desolated about everything.

The gesture aged me so much that Monsieur Saint-Hilaire laughed as at the most absurd spectacle he'd ever seen.

"Well—so what then?" he asked.

"Well, so this summer my mother couldn't find the money."

"Your mother finds money then?" the old man interrupted.

"Sometimes, when we need it really badly."

"And does she find it by searching?"

"Oh no," I said, smiling a little, for I had suddenly pictured Maman, lamp in hand, searching in dark corners. "No, it isn't that she searches, but she does find money sometimes. Only not this time. And it costs quite a lot," I explained, "to send me by train to the country where my relatives are. We're lucky. We have several uncles who are farmers. Maman thought one or another of them might come to town by car on business at the beginning of the holidays; I could have gone back with him. That wouldn't have cost us a cent; it would have been all to the good. But none of them came. And now it's too late; they'll all be busy soon with the threshing. They won't be coming now till it's time to shop for the winter. Hope, for this summer at least, is dead."

"Tut, tut, tut. You must never say that hope is dead. Hope never dies."

"No?" I said a little more joyfully. "It never dies?"

"Not to my knowledge, in any event."

And now it appeared to be certain, since he who must know all about such things, said so.

Then he asked me, "The country where your uncles live, what sort of country is it?"

"Oh, it's beautiful!"

"Well! As beautiful as all that!"

This was a subject of which I was very fond; like the heat, it was always worth ninety-eight or ninety-nine marks to me in my compositions at school.

"The country of my uncles," I began after a deep breath, as if I were going to continue for a long time and say many things, and discovered at that moment, alas, that I couldn't do justice to what I loved . . . but I went on just the same. "It's much higher than it is here. In attitude," I explained.

"Altitude," corrected the old man.

"Altitude," I repeated. "And the air is good there. It is brisk. When I arrive at my uncles, I eat twice as much as I do here and I find everything good."

I thought for a moment, my chin in my hands. I remembered with pleasure a charming grove of young aspens that surrounded my uncle Cléophas's house, its murmurs filling all the summer days, making me exclaim a little sadly when I got up in the morning, "Oh it's raining," whereupon everyone made fun of the little city dweller who did not yet know how to distinguish the sound of rain from the essentially rather similar sound of the too sensitive leaves as they were set in motion by the least breath of air. "Why, no," I was told. "It's a beautiful day. That's only the wind in the aspens." . . . "But the wind isn't blowing." . . . "Yes, it is in the aspens. Listen . . ."

I must have smiled at the memory, for the old man asked me to tell him what I was thinking. I was going to tell him and talk about the mischievous young wood that played the same trick on me each summer, no matter how used to it I should have been, and made me believe it was raining. But suddenly I changed my mind, struck by another memory, and spoke instead of the wheat fields.

For as soon as you came out of this wood at my uncle's, you found yourself on the edge of an immense plain, quite open and almost entirely in crops. So that at my uncle's I never knew which I liked best—the grove of aspens that sheltered us, served as a hiding place, and made us feel at home, or the great spread-out land that seemed to summon us to voyages. As my uncle said, both had charm, one reposing from the other.

"Do you know," I said, "that my uncle Cléophas has almost a square mile in wheat?"

"That's a great deal."

"Yes, it is a great deal, and, when the wheat is tall and strong, we play hide-and-seek in it. I'm almost never found."

"I don't doubt it," said the old man with a rather troubled look. For he asked, "Running roughshod like that through the lovely wheat, doesn't that crush it?"

"A little . . . and my uncle doesn't always allow it. . . . But that doesn't matter."

For when the wheat had reached its full height, I no longer needed to rush about to be happy. In those expanses too, the slightest wind set up a gentle oscillating movement. It was enough then simply to look at it, small beside its great unfurled expanse, and listen to its rustle.

I sighed.

"This summer I'll see nothing of all that."

The old man also sighed.

Perhaps we were chiefly sighing in astonishment at finding ourselves suddenly back again on the bald bit of grass in our cramped little corner.

"From what you tell me it must indeed be pleasant where

your uncles live," the old man agreed. "But doesn't it perhaps lack water? Is there at least a little somewhere?"

"Water?"

I searched among my memories.

"Because in the dog days," said the old man, "when the intense heat comes, it's very nice to look at."

The dog days, I thought, enchanted by this new expression. With my old man, I was learning something every day.

"There's the well," I said.

"Yes, of course, the well."

I searched further.

"It seems to me . . . it seems to me . . . that one day when we all went out in the old Ford, all my uncle's family, to pick saskatoons over toward Manitou . . . it seems to me that that time I may have seen a lake."

"Was it really a lake?" asked the old man. "Wouldn't it have been one of those coulees . . . such as one sees over there?"

"Perhaps it was only a coulee. . . ."

"What would its extent have been?"

"Its ex . . . what?"

Then I believed I understood.

"Oh, it was certainly as big as from here to the other side of the street."

"Then it must have been only a coulee. You've never seen Lake Winnipeg?" he asked.

"No, only in my geography book. Have you seen it?"

"When I was young," said the old man, "I used to make the trip almost every summer especially to see it."

"That must have been a long time ago."

The old man closed his eyes.

"Yes, it was a long time ago."

"And the lake hasn't changed since then?"

He smiled benevolently.

"A lake doesn't change. At least not in the course of a human life . . . or even of several generations."

"Ah, it doesn't change any more than that! It must be old too. . . ."

"Why no, on the contrary, it's always young."

"Ah!"

"The world is young," he told me.

"Ah!"

I was astonished, having always heard and repeated the expression "as old as the world."

"And what is Lake Winnipeg like?" I asked him.

"Oh, it's quite a thing to see," said the old man. "It's really quite a thing to see."

"And it's very big?"

"Tremendously big."

"When you're at one end of it, can you see to the other end?"

"No, precisely," said the old man. "You can't see from one shore to the other. It's too vast."

"Vast," I echoed dreamily. "And it's nothing but water?"

"Nothing but water."

"Always water?"

"Always water."

"And that's beautiful, so much water?"

"I wonder if I've ever seen anything more beautiful."

"And does this water speak, and sing, and say something?"

"Yes," said the old man, pleased with my question. "This water, as you put it so nicely, speaks and sings and says something incessantly, even though you can't hear anything clearly as you do when people speak, for instance. And also, it's best to keep very quiet if you wish to hear the lake."

"Incessantly, incessantly?"

"Yes, incessantly, I think. It's a little like your immense fields of wheat, my little chicken. Have you ever come upon them when they were absolutely silent?"

"Hardly ever."

"It's the same with water. At the tiniest caress of the air, it stirs, forms little waves, and dances and splashes in the sun."

"It would be nice to be there now," I said.

"Oh yes, it would be very nice!"

Then we fell silent, our throats dry, dazed with the heat, seeing in our aching heads the rise and fall of limpid water.

3

This morning Maman returned precipitately from her usual brief sally onto the gallery.

"It's atrocious," she said. "It will certainly go up over a hundred today. Don't anyone go out. On the stroke of noon we'll make ourselves some sandwiches to take down with us in the cellar for lunch."

This prospect, which might offer itself two or three times in a summer, usually enchanted me. But today I couldn't think of anything but Lake Winnipeg and learning as much about it as I could.

By dint of pleading and coaxing, I finally convinced my mother that I would be better outside than in the cellar and she let me go out, first fetching me from the attic an old farmer's straw hat, which fell down over my face, hiding it almost completely.

Thus protected, I ran to the old man. He and his maple tree were as if in a picture. Nothing stirred, neither on the earth nor in the expanse of the sky. Even the eyes of the poor old man looked dry. There was no longer the slightest trace of moisture on the old fissured soil of his face; I daresay it had not a single further drop to spare.

"Sit down and keep very still," he advised me. "This heat is strong enough to kill everything, except perhaps ideas of coolness."

This was precisely the sort of thing I had wished to hear.

"Has Lake Winnipeg also an ext . . . ent?" I asked.

"An extent? Yes, of course. At its point of greatest length, it must be considerably more than two hundred miles. But don't trust me for figures and statistics. Funny things happen when one gets old, you know. For instance, you will forever afterward remember a certain red dress you saw someone wear one day, or a pot of geraniums you glimpsed as you passed through a city, you no longer know which—odd little details like that. Figures, on the other hand, went right out of my head a long time ago."

I laughed, because I imagined a whole row of figures coming swiftly out of the dear old man's head and beginning to run and flutter through the air.

Then I exclaimed, "Two hundred miles! Think of that! That's much farther even than it is to my uncles'. So you could travel for a whole day on the lake and not arrive anywhere."

"You certainly wouldn't get far in a rowboat," said the old man. "Or even in a motorboat."

As on the previous day, I was crouching on the ground at his feet. From between the blades of scanty yellow grass I was gathering up handfuls of the exposed soil, which was fine and dusty as sand, and letting it trickle between my fingers.

"In Saskatchewan," I informed him, "it's even worse, it seems, than here. All the soil has turned to dust like this"—

and I showed him what I had in my hand. "It is flying in the wind. Saskatchewan is going to become a desert," I repeated, in the solemn tone in which I had heard the words spoken.

"A desert! Perhaps . . ."

I had thought it all right to take off my rustic straw hat, since I was sitting in the shade. The old man stretched out his hand and took up a lock of my hair, which he studied as if it were something quite unusual.

"I wonder . . ." he began, then apparently changed his mind and went on to another subject, which was perhaps related to the first since he could introduce it in the same way. "I wonder," he said, "what your mother thinks of me."

I told him at one go, without shame or embarrassment.

"Oh, she thinks you're a very proper old gentleman but with stubborn ideas."

This was the first time I had heard him laugh exactly as grown-up people do, with a trace of malice and all sorts of undertones.

"Your mother's judgment isn't at all bad."

The next day again he repeated his curious introductory phrase, "I wonder . . ." and again went no further.

It was only on the third attempt that he went right to the end.

"I wonder if your mother would trust you to me for a whole day. We could take the train and go to see Lake Winnipeg."

Immediately I was on my feet. I leaped like an excited goat.

"There, there now, be careful, don't rejoice too quickly," said the old man. "If your mother won't let you, what will you do then, my little chicken?"

What would I do? It was as if I'd suddenly plunged down

seven or eight stories. But how, in such a short time, had I
been able to mount so high?

"You see!" he said. "You mustn't climb too high too quickly.
You mustn't count your chickens before they're hatched.
It's bad for the heart, my pretty one. It's well to look into
things a bit first."

"But I want to go to the lake with you," I cried, almost in
tears.

"Yes, I know," said the old man. "I myself have thought
of nothing else for a whole week. We're a fine pair. For it's
quite a little trip. We wouldn't be able to come back till after
nightfall. I've consulted the timetable and there's no help
for it. The train doesn't return from Winnipeg Beach till
almost eleven. On the other hand," he said dreamily, "your
mother looks like a person of intuition, who can see beyond
conventionalities and preformed judgments. She looks like a
woman of inspiration. . . ."

It was with this fine, slightly impenetrable word that I
returned home in due course.

I ran to Maman in the cellar, threw my arms around her
neck, and said cajolingly, "You are a woman of inspiration."

"Really!" she said.

"Of inspiration!" I cried, disappointed that she was not
more delighted by a compliment of such rarity. So I couldn't
help giving its source, thinking that then she would understand its value. "It's true. It was Monsieur Saint-Hilaire who
said so."

My poor mother! I don't suppose I had even thought till
then that she had never seen Lake Winnipeg either, though
it is not far from where we lived. But, always the slave to
our needs, when and how could she have yielded for even a
day to the still eager desires of her own spirit—those wide-

ranging desires that were turned always toward water, toward the open plains, and toward those distant horizons which alone reveal to us some part of our truest selves? And was she not beginning to realize that for her it was late now and not much time remained to appease those longings that, if not satisfied, leave us as if imperfect in our own eyes, in a train of nostalgic regrets? But for this reason she had become vigilant to obtain for us, at least, the things she had not possessed of this world.

She pricked up her ears at my first words. Exhausted as she was, she smiled at my extraordinary enthusiasm.

"Beautiful Lake Winnipeg, Maman!"

She looked at me and, as almost always happened, forgot her own rights in favor of mine.

"How sickly and thin you look," she said, seeing it better than ever perhaps, just because I was so animated, "a big fire of little faggots," as was often said of me. "These holidays haven't done you much good, poor child." And she took up her daily sewing. "Oh if only I could have sent you to the country! I could have, of course, but only by using money that might be needed even more somewhere else. Though how does one know what is most important?"

Absorbed in her own thoughts, she was not paying attention to what I was telling her so volubly. "So the old gentleman wants to take me to spend a whole day at the lake. . . ."

Then, instinctively, I changed "the old gentleman" to "dear Monsieur Saint-Hilaire."

Maman was finally listening to me.

"This Monsieur Saint-Hilaire of yours," she said with a touch of envy. "His name is always on your lips. What more has he dreamed up, that old child?"

I went back to my pleading, expressing myself badly, I know, in the frenzy of my desire, out of fear of not doing it justice, for I hadn't failed to realize that this was not the sort of thing one could ask for every day. For the skill I lacked, I substituted intensity.

"Maman, the biggest lake in Manitoba . . . perhaps in the world! And I will never have seen it! I too will have lived my whole life without seeing it!"

Maman understood at last. Her eyebrows were knotted and her eyes set, but even so she began to smile a little at my dreadful pessimism.

"Oh, your whole life! What is your whole life to you now? Believe me, you have plenty of time before you need to start renouncing."

Then she became anxious, anxious as I have seldom seen her to be, she who had so much to be anxious about. She was sitting on a log in the dark cellar, close to the big furnace, which was dead now, of course. And it was at once sad and comic to see her trying to find a little coolness beside this furnace, which in wintertime was so hot that no one chose to come near it but the cat.

"Those two together for a whole day," she said to herself. "And not coming back till night—"

"That's because of the train," I explained quickly.

"Whose idea was this?" she asked with some severity. "Yours?"

"Oh no, no no no."

She softened slightly. I gave her then a little caress, trying to rub out with my fingers some small wrinkles I had suddenly discovered at the corners of her eyes.

"This is one of the most annoying problems I have ever had to solve," she said.

My petulance and fear returned.

"I don't see what's so annoying about it."

"You don't understand."

I saw her eyes stray toward the pile of coal in the corner

and settle upon the things that surrounded it, all the various winter things—a snow shovel, some corded wood, a hand-saw—as if they could help her to make up her mind. Her eyes hardened as if for a refusal, then, as I watched, they grew first hesitant, then tender and acquired a gleam of consent.

I was on pins and needles. I felt that these arguments would kill me.

"Ah, say yes, Maman. It's only for a day."

"I don't know what I should do," she admitted.

Seeing her shaken, I clutched her by the arm, then pushed her a little so I could sit beside her on the log.

"Maman, beautiful Lake Winnipeg that I haven't ever seen in my whole life!"

Usually she laughed at me when I said such things. This time she appeared to be touched. Had she put herself in the place of the child whose desire amounted almost to pain? Or put me in the place of the aging mother who perhaps would never see the lake?

"I haven't the time or the money to take you to see it my-self," she said by way of an excuse, as if her conscience abso-lutely required that there be one.

Then she looked at me, undecided again, and yet lured and drawn herself, I do believe, by the mirage of open water that seemed to have come right into the somber musty-smell-ing cellar to fill our imaginations.

Did she wish to see at least something of the lake in my eyes when I returned? Or was she thinking throughout chiefly of the old man, who had not much more time in which to see it again? In any case her prudence seemed to be in flight, her prudence which, much more than many others—and God be praised for this—she was able to set aside sometimes, in order, as she expressed it, "to give way to the folly of my nature."

4

We set out early in the morning, for this once mocking at the heat and even hoping, I believe, without a thought for those who must remain in the city, that it would be more intense than ever, since this would make our coolness beside the lake even more desirable.

"It would be quite disastrous," the old man said as we arrived at the station, "if today of all days the air should freshen and perhaps turn to rain. But I don't think they'll play such a nasty trick on us. Something tells me that today will be the summit of this monstrous heat wave. It may go up to a hundred and two degrees. But we'll hardly notice it at the lake."

We took our places on the train, the old man installing me beside the window so I should miss none of the landscape.

I was wearing my pink organdy dress and a big bow of white ribbon in my hair. Maman had carefully instructed me not to begin to fuss or to try to tease the old man to buy me this or that. She had instructed him in turn not to give in to my whims or let me eat too much ice cream or popcorn.

Aside from this, she had abandoned us willingly to our mysterious tenderness, just saying with her eyes, it seems to me: I'm a fool, there's no doubt of that. It can't be imagined what a fool I am to let you go.

At any rate, believing I had interpreted Maman's wishes very well, I was as attentive to the old man from the time we set out as he was to me.

Soon the train gave a little shake that delighted me. But this was only a maneuver. We remained in the station for five long minutes more; impatiently I shifted with my hips against the seat, perhaps trying to urge the train to leave. Finally it happened. At once, I believe, with my eyes glued to the window, I began to watch for the appearance of the lake.

The old man laughed at my nervous excitement.

"Try to calm down," he said. "Impatience is exhausting. At this rate you'll be worn out before you've even seen the lake. You'll have nothing left to give the very thing that deserves the most. Is that the way you want to be when you reach the lake?"

Ah no, I thought. I must certainly save myself for the lake.

"We still have almost two hours to go before we arrive," he said. "That may seem long but, you'll see, it will pass. Save yourself for the lake."

I managed to stop shifting my legs, my shoulders, and my arms. But inside me all was still shakes, leaps, and jumps. My heart was bounding like a little caged animal that knows someone will open the door for him. In his longing for the door to be opened, he runs in all directions, thumps all over, unable to contain himself, to say to himself, "But the door is going to open." From time to time I pressed my hand against that part of myself where such curious things were taking place.

The old man understood that I was so happy I was sick with it. He smiled at me with infinite patience. He admitted that when he was my age, when there was going to be a picnic, for instance, he used to spend himself ahead of time with the same exhausting frenzy, that children were all alike in this, which was, when you really thought of it, a curious thing.

"Why is it," he asked, "that those who have all the time in the world ahead of them feel such a need to hurry?"

I didn't know. All I knew was that I was anxious to hurry.

"Yet the mountains and lakes wait," he said. "They remain in their places. They can't do anything else but wait."

Perhaps, I thought, but Maman, who has waited with all the patience in the world, is still in the cellar looking at the sky through the ventilator. For the first time I didn't entirely agree with my old friend. If one doesn't hurry terribly, I told myself, many things get away from us, even those that remain motionless to wait for us.

We were traveling through a sad little forest of frail gray trees—perhaps they were not even trees, but just tangled bushes with which were mingled a few firs and some rather lifeless spruce trees. Or perhaps it was one of those forests that have been destroyed by fire and are growing back weakly. In any event, like me, the old man found this region, which he called a savanna, rather depressing.

It was almost as hot as in the center of the city. How could the air have circulated through these thick but puny little woods? Only speed created air. I had my head out of the coach most of the time, trying to catch a trace of wind on my face. But the old man begged me to pull my head back in, pointing out that it could be dangerous to leave it outside.

I obeyed him. Maman had told me to obey him. Quite on my own, as well, I felt that, child as the old man was, I still owed him obedience—and also protection. When you examine them closely, our relations were curious, very curious indeed —yet were they not infinitely clear?

After I had obeyed him, I searched my imagination for a long time for something I might be able to get him to do for his good, but I could find nothing.

Then suddenly the train gave a bold and joyous whistle, as if it were announcing: Watch now, you're about to see something marvelous, new, and worthwhile! At the same time it made a rather quick sharp turn. I saw then—or believed I saw—an immense sheet of tender blue, deep, glossy, and, it seemed to me, liquid. My soul stretched wide to receive it.

"It's the lake?"

The old man had seen my eyes grow large, my hands reach out toward this open blue.

"It's only the sky," he said.

After a long silence, I asked, "Are they alike?"

The old man nodded pensively.

"Yes, the lake and the sky are essentially alike. At times they are exactly the same color."

"Always blue?"

"No, not always blue. Far from that. The lake takes its mood from the sky. If the sky is gray and taciturn, the lake is also gray and taciturn."

"But why does the sky become taciturn? Is it unhappy?"

"Yes, that might be it," said the old man with a rather absent smile.

Then he became more animated again.

"Even so, when the lake is angry, it is a lovely thing to see."

"When it's angry?"

"Ah yes! Suppose a violent wind springs up. Soon the lake too is completely agitated. Then the wind becomes more and more stormy. Now the lake is the color of lead. A little more time and it rocks from side to side. On Lake Winnipeg," he told me, "I have seen storms almost as great as on the ocean."

"Ah! The ocean!" I said. "That's another thing I haven't seen in my whole life. So many things I haven't seen!"

"Hey there!" the old man stopped me. "Be content for today with Lake Winnipeg. Believe me, it's quite enough for one day. You mustn't wish to gobble life up."

"Yes," I agreed. "Lake Winnipeg should be enough for one day. But tell me again what it's like when the strong wind blows."

"That depends," said the old man, "on what side the wind is blowing from and whether the day is otherwise fair or gloomy. Would you like me to tell you about one of the times when the lake seemed to me most beautiful?"

"Oh yes, tell me about that time."

"That day," he said, "the lake was covered with millions of waves, not very high but swift and running from all directions. Each wore a white crest. One might have thought they were birds letting themselves be carried and rocked by the waves. And some real birds, little lake gulls, had settled on the rough water and they too were incessantly rising and falling, yet holding themselves still, with their grayish wings pasted to their bodies and their brightly colored beaks sparkling. The lake that day seemed to me to be dancing before the Lord."

Ah, how that image pleased me! I could see them—the gulls or the waves, I wasn't sure which—equally white and bounding. I was so violently excited at that moment that the old man took my wrist and searched for my pulse, which was so fast, he told me, that he could scarcely count it.

"It's like a little watch gone crazy," he told me, as if he were scolding.

It was not my fault, however. Already, because of this too active pulse, I had been forbidden violent exercise, and if I had learned to walk on stilts just the same, it was unbeknownst to Maman.

"Are you going to be as passionate as this all your life?" the old man asked me.

How could I know? Nevertheless I replied coolly, "Yes, I shall be like this all my life."

Then the old man teased me a little.

"Since my stories have such an effect upon you," he said, "I shan't tell you any more."

But a few minutes later he did tell me others. That the lake, for instance, was older than the soil of Manitoba and that it would still be there when millions of years had passed. For the eternity of time, he told me.

I felt suddenly afraid at these words, disturbed as I was when I went into the little grove of somber oak trees, where I always found—but why there?—the memory of my grandmother in her coffin.

"The eternity of time—that's when you die," I said.

"Why no, it's eternal life," said the old man.

I understood even less, but it didn't matter, for at that moment the train took a rather sharp curve and we were flung together toward the aisle, which made us laugh with delight. Then the train whistled. The woods opened out wide. Blue appeared, still far away, but even at this distance I sensed it was alive.

"There it is!" I cried, rising and putting my hand on my heart once more in that curious, little old woman's gesture I had had since childhood.

Then I turned my eyes to the old man.

He nodded. He too was much too happy to speak. But his eyes were no longer watching the great open stretch of water spread out in the distance. They were watching me instead, as if I were the huge lake we had come to see.

5

After this free glimpse of the lake, Winnipeg Beach disillusioned me to the point of bitter tears. Somewhere in the sky I could see a circus wheel turning, and from all sides came the intermingled cries of street hawkers, the tinkling of cheap music, and the odor of hot grease. In the distance the little cars of the roller coaster rushed downhill, full of people from whom came, after a breathless silence, a long hysterical shriek. Alas, we were still in a town, which had streets, close-packed shops, and swarming restaurants, but a very much sadder town than ours; here people walked about half-naked, a towel over their shoulders, eating fried potatoes from paper cornets or hot sausages on rolls.

I seized the old man's hand, whimpering, "The lake? Where's the lake?"

"Patience," he said. "We'll get there, we'll get there."

We circled unhappily for a long time, however, seeking for a way out of this crowd that jostled us about and once or twice almost separated us from each other.

"Nothing is as it was in my time," the old man muttered. "It's incredible. In my time there was nothing here but a wooden station and, a bit farther along, a dozen or so little cottages. Ah, the wretches, to spoil the countryside for us like this."

Seeing him so baffled, I felt plunged into a sense of catastrophe. I began to have doubts, I think, of what he'd told me about the lake. Perhaps none of it was true any more. I was so anxious about the things he had promised me that I clutched him by the arm.

"Will we at least be able to find it?" I asked.

"Find what, little one?"

"The lake."

"Ah, that!" and he returned to himself—or should I say, rather, to me?—and laughed a little. "Such a big lake! They can't have taken it somewhere else, though they'd have been quite capable of trying to if they could."

"Ah good!" I said, slightly cheered, but not understanding who it was that would have tried to attack the lake if they could.

"Scoundrels, scoundrels," grumbled the old man. I had never seen him even slightly angry before, and it astonished me greatly. "One thing though," he said. "The little town looks to me to be quite far from the beach. Suppose we eat now before we get too far away. Or shall we first go and find the lake?"

"Oh, let's find the lake!"

He pressed my hand gently.

"I knew that was what you'd want."

Gradually we left the odor of frying and the cries of the fairground behind us. We were still going along streets but now they were of sand. Then the sidewalks also ceased. The cottages on either side became more and more hidden among spruce and firs, which smelled good in the sun. I studied the slightest reaction of the old man, still greatly astonished at seeing him so peevish.

"Is it now as in your time?" I asked.

For an impossible desire had come over me, to see his time—which I imagined perhaps as resembling him—restored to him now. But I had such doubts of the possible realization of such a wish that I went on with apprehension, "Times, things like that, can they be found again?"

"Sometimes . . . sometimes . . ." he murmured, at first as if he were not at all sure, then gradually as if he did actually believe it might happen after all.

For at that moment there came from somewhere ahead of us a fresh breeze that was even brisker than the air of the open prairie. This brisk air took us by surprise. We raised our heads, looking at each other as we drank it in.

"That's its breath," the old man told me.

An instant later he stopped me with a hand on my shoulder. "Listen. You can hear it."

That was true. Before we saw it, we could hear it—a great regular beating like hands applauding in the distance. At once I longed to run ahead. But the old man was having trouble walking in the soft sand. He was already out of breath. So I tried to wait for him, all the while pulling a little at his hand.

At last we came to a long beach of a sand that was as tender to the feet as to the sight. Ahead of us, from one horizon to the other, as the old man had said, was the lake. Nothing but water. But there was something else I had not expected: this was that the lake, even while it made its particular sound heard, also kept silent. How could these be reconciled—this impression of a tireless murmur and, at the same time, of silence? Seemingly I still haven't managed to do it, in all the time I have given to the subject, since this visit to the first great lake of my life. I wonder even whether I am any further ahead now than I was that day.

We sat down side by side in the sand before Lake Winnipeg. The gentle waves came almost to our feet, to whisper perhaps that they were happy to see us here at last. I began to look for gulls on the waves, but there were none as yet. A marvelous freshness constantly touched our faces. For a long moment—a half hour perhaps—we wanted nothing else but to give ourselves up to watching and listening to the lake.

At length the old man asked me, "Are you happy?"

I was undoubtedly happier than I had ever been before, but, as if it were too great, this unknown joy held me in a state of intense astonishment. I learned later on, of course, that this is the very essence of joy, this astonished delight, this sense of a revelation at once so simple, so natural, and yet so great that one doesn't quite know what to say of it, except, "Ah, so this is it."

All my preparations had been useless; everything surpassed my expectations, this great sky, half cloudy and half sunlit, this incredible crescent of beach, the water, above all, its boundless expanse, which to my land-dweller's eyes, accustomed to parched horizons, must have seemed somewhat wasteful, trained as we were to hoard water. I could not get over it. Have I, moreover, ever got over it? Does one ever, fundamentally, get over a great lake?

Despite the tender caress of the breeze, we quickly realized that the sun struck hard on this widespread sand. At his age, the old man told me, nothing was so much to be feared as excess, an excess of sun like any other—and certainly, it seemed to me, this had been a summer of excess. He took a folded newspaper from his pocket and made himself a sort of cocked hat. The air would circulate better, he told me, than under his hat from the Caribbees, which would benefit, in any case, from a quiet rest on the beach. He saw that I was anxious to have a hat like his, so he took the cocked hat apart, divided the paper, and had enough to make a new hat for himself and a smaller one for me.

Then, similarly capped, with the hat from the Caribbees between us on the sand, we looked exactly what we were, little folk from the city who were unaccustomed to the ways of beaches and had come there only to dream.

More and more people overran the beach. They were for the most part young, bronzed, and laughing; they ran barefoot over the sand or went to throw themselves into the water with a great resounding splash. We kept our secret Sunday air. I don't think it ever occurred to me that I might look as if I had anything to complain about, sitting stiff in my organdy dress beside an old man in black. If by chance the glances we attracted embarrassed me, I think the tranquil breathing of the lake, the grandeur and perfection all around me would quickly have managed to dispel such a paltry feeling as pride. Maman, it is true, had regretted that, since I was going to the lake for the day, she couldn't buy me a bathing suit and hadn't time to make me something to take its place—and she could have done it, for she was clever with her hands. She had suggested that I could at least hitch up my dress and paddle in the water a little. I don't think I felt any desire to do this. In the first place, this was my new dress. And furthermore, in the sun under my cocked hat, with the moist coolness bathing my face incessantly and my dear old friend as companion, I seemed to have everything that mattered—a happiness so rare that I must be careful not to place too much weight on it lest I mar its delicate fabric.

"You can go and play," the old man told me.

I shook my head. A day like today seemed to me as little made for games—those, at least, that I knew—as, for instance, a day in church with its organ music and jubilation. I amused myself simply by gathering up the lovely clean dry sand and letting it slip between my fingers, or making little mounds of it and packing their bases and sides down well.

All this time the deep song of the lake penetrated me. I heard clearly now that it was not in the least like the sound of hands striking against each other in a full hall on the night of a concert. A short distance away I could see a long thin breaker form and rush toward the shore, where it broke with a sort of sigh that was perhaps a little sad. There followed a fraction of a second of silence, and then the water spread gently over the sand, making another damp and fresher stain. Was it the same breaker that constantly made and unmade itself? Or did they come endlessly from the bottom of the lake?

I asked the old man, who told me he didn't know, he who always took such pains to answer my questions. I looked at him for a moment in stupefaction, wondering what could have happened to him. He was "curdling," according to an expression of Maman's, by which she meant the vagueness that comes into the gaze when, through weariness and the need for sleep, the attention is no longer fixed; and it is true that at such moments you can see it thicken suddenly as does milk on a hot day. Undoubtedly, deranged in all his little regular habits, he must have felt a great need for sleep, and I should have left him undisturbed under his cocked newspaper hat, which swayed a little with the nodding of his head—today I still regret not having let him sleep. But at the time eager questions crowded upon me. Why so much water? And why all in one place and none at all elsewhere? And why the waves?

The weary old man shook himself. He forced himself to give me what I wanted.

"Why so much water? For its beauty, I imagine. Because God decided it that way."

"Then he made Lake Winnipeg for himself?"

"For himself? Yes, I daresay," said the old man. "But for us also."

"He knew we'd be coming to see it?"

Even weary as he was, the old man smiled a little.

"He must have suspected that we would."

All this time I was straining my eyes, trying to make out, beyond the vibrations of the light on the water, the end of the lake, its far-off banks.

"Over there, over there?" I asked. "Is that the end or the beginning?"

I had finally succeeded in rousing the old man from his

somnolence and I was delighted to see his little blue eyes come to life, though they had a rather sad expression at the moment.

"The end or the beginning? Such questions you ask! The end or the beginning. And if they are fundamentally the same . . ."

He was also looking into the distance as he spoke, and now repeated, "If they are the same . . . Perhaps everything finally forms a great circle, the end and the beginning coming together."

I liked him to talk to me at times in this elevated tone, with words whose sound, even if I did not comprehend the full sense, pleased me as did symphonic music or the sight, high in the sky, of those dreamy passing clouds which seem to represent something, we are not sure what.

I now remembered that he had told me the lake was longer than it was wide. I asked him whether, since the lake was not round, the beginning and the end could still touch each other. He replied that this did not change the mysterious encounter in any way, that the end and the beginning had their own way of finding each other.

Now hundreds of bathers were playing, chasing each other with sharp cries, throwing water in each other's faces, or tossing beach balls through the surf. We were the only ones who appeared to be completely unoccupied.

"It doesn't tempt you to go and play?"

I shook my head. I was still struggling to distinguish the slightly melancholy song of the water as it came to spread itself upon the sand. When the shouts and the joyful uproar of the crowd diminished slightly, I could hear it, tranquil, always the same. Now it seemed to be a little whispered phrase. Had the lake had only this one thing to say since the beginning of time, I wondered, and repeated it over and over again. Was it speaking particularly to me or would it have spoken to others too if they had listened? Then finally, as I tried to make out what it was saying, the little whispered phrase lulled me half to sleep. I stretched out in spite of myself; in spite of myself I surrendered to the same little phrase whose meaning I should have so much liked to know.

But just as I was about to fall asleep, the old man completely wakened.

"Aren't you hungry now?" he asked. "You must be. Shall we think at last about eating?"

At once I was on my feet, discovering, in fact, that the fresh air had given me an excellent appetite.

"I could eat for ten," I said.

"So much the better," said the old man.

We went back, by a path through the sand, then a plank sidewalk, finally a cement pavement, to the little town, where luckily we found a restaurant that wasn't too crowded, as the old man had wished. When I realized that despite my mother's instructions he was going to order me a banana and marshmallow sundae, I could scarcely keep from exclaiming that he was the best friend I had ever had in my life. He tied my table napkin around my neck, so I wouldn't stain my pretty pink dress, he said.

"It's the prettiest I have," I told him, "and at first Maman wouldn't hear of my wearing it to sit in the sand."

"But you wanted to show it to the lake, I suppose," said the old man, winking at me.

Perhaps that was it.

"Actually you were quite right," said the old man approvingly. "One puts on one's prettiest dress for tiresome ceremonies. Why shouldn't one also put it on for a day of splendor?"

I instructed him in turn to be very careful not to soil his black poplin coat, in which he always looked so neat and which made him so well thought of, I told him, by everyone in our town. Half in fun, half serious, I helped him place his table napkin high enough to cover his beard, since it was also very neat and clean. Suddenly overcome with curiosity, I thought of finding out whether he had to wash it with shampoo like his hair. This simple question made him laugh till he almost choked, though I saw nothing in the matter to cause such amusement.

No, he told me, he merely wiped it with a slightly dampened cloth and then combed it. Sometimes he gave it a touch with the brush to finish it off. But there was no doubt that a beard was a bit of a worry, if only because it had a tendency to catch the fragments that fell from the mouth. So those people who imagined that a beard was a lazy man's habit were mistaken. Keeping one's beard clean was even more work than shaving.

"And it's handsome besides," I said.

This seemed to give him pleasure.

"Do you think so?"

"Oh yes, and it's unusual!"

"That's true. It's beginning to be unusual in our day."

While we were looking after each other like this and speaking heart to heart, people at neighboring tables were watching us. They seemed delighted with us both, and perhaps a little bit envious. Then a lady, who believed she was speaking softly or that the noise of dishes would cover her voice, said quite audibly, "Isn't it charming to see a grandfather and granddaughter together and getting along so well?"

We exchanged a look that sparkled with what we knew: that we were not really grandfather and granddaughter, and yet we were, in a sense, even more than if we had really been so in fact.

A little later, the old man became thoughtful. He turned

his spoon endlessly in his cup. He told me that he had grand-children of his own—who were no longer small, however—that they weren't unkind or heartless but suffered from the malady of the times: a fondness for speed and cars and motorcycles and also for spending money as quickly as they could . . . and that he felt too old now to be able to adapt himself to the frenzy of the day.

Yet to me he seemed very well able to adapt himself. When I had emptied my sundae cup and scraped the bottom a little, I became thoughtful in my turn.

"Because," I told him, "I no longer have a grandfather or a grandmother or anyone."

"What do you mean 'or anyone'?" he said, as if I had vexed him.

Perhaps this wasn't exactly what I had intended to say. Yet for a moment I had seen my grandmother as she had been when she sometimes argued but always sewed so beauti-fully and the idea that she was no longer sewing anywhere now had made me feel forsaken.

"It is true," said the old man, "that when a single person is lacking, the world can seem to be a desert."

Then he blew his nose and said, "But that's not the way it is with us, is it?"

I also blew my nose. I was suddenly not so sure that wasn't the way it was with us, but I agreed with him to give him pleasure.

Then he began to "curdle" once more. He even slept for a while finally, after murmuring that it was stronger than he, sleep always lay in wait for him after meals.

I watched him sleeping without making a sound for a few minutes. The restaurant had gradually emptied. We were quite alone, and now that there was no more noise around us, the place made me feel a great desire to be gone. I heard a fly bumping against the ceiling. Then the old man began to snore faintly. It was sad, this low whistling that escaped his partly opened lips. His denture slipped a little way out of his mouth. He seemed very much older suddenly than he had ever seemed to me before, no doubt because his blue eyes were always so lively when he was awake. But at present, with only a bit of milky white showing under the half-closed lids, they frightened me. I could no longer recognize him. Then one of his hands, which had been lying on the table-cloth, slipped from the table, fell the length of his body and remained there, dangling and dead-looking. I was afraid. I reached out my fingers to touch that inert hand, and it had much the effect on me as a dead bird I had found one day and taken in my hands. I don't know what possessed me then— the thought perhaps that the old man would never wake up again unless I hurried to bring him back from that other side. Who knows what thoughts went through my mind?

I began to call his name. "Monsieur Saint-Hilaire! Monsieur Saint-Hilaire!"

Maman's hesitation about letting us go off together now seemed justified, and I thought I understood that it was on the old man's account rather than on mine that she had feared the journey so much.

"Monsieur Saint-Hilaire!"

He jumped, opened his eyes, and seemed not to know where he was or who I was. For those few seconds it was as if he were looking at me from a greater distance than if the whole of Lake Winnipeg lay between us. I had never been looked at from so far away by someone I knew, and in a way this frightened me even more than seeing him asleep. At last he recognized me and smiled as if reassured.

"It's you, my little friend! You did well to wake me up. I fall asleep at every turn these days and wake up completely lost."

"Don't fall asleep again," I begged.

He shook the crumbs from his beard, paid his bill, and said, as we were leaving, "You're right . . . this is not a day to sleep. I'll have time enough for that, believe me!"

Then he managed to pull himself together fairly well and said, "So. We still have a few hours of daylight left. . . . Shall we make use of them to go back to the lake?"

"Oh yes. Let's go back to the lake," I said.

So, hand in hand, keeping close to each other like people who feared to be separated but saying little more to each other, we returned, a little sadly and slowly, toward that great friendly murmur in the distance, which once again, even before we had reached it, we could hear coming to meet us.

This time we had the long beach of fine sand almost to ourselves. The weather had changed. Heavy menacing clouds were coming from that far-off part of the lake into which I had gazed, wondering whether it was the end or the beginning. A gust of wind passed over us. But instead of breaking into the lovely little waves I longed to see, the water merely wrinkled and took on an evil gray color. I was astonished that the lake, so radiant in the sun, could look so morose. Then the air cooled brusquely. We almost shivered.

"You won't take cold now?" said the old man anxiously. "You should have brought along a sweater. But who'd have thought you'd need it this morning when we set out?"

Then we began to speak of our home as "there," and as if it were already years since we had left it.

"I wonder if the weather has freshened there too," said the old man. "Perhaps not. It's so changeable here. But there it may still be a steam bath."

We had found the same place to sit on the sand; I had recognized it by the series of little pyramids I had erected. I continued to make others, but without much enthusiasm.

"They must feel there," I said, and I was also thinking of our hot and stifling little streets, "as if we've been away for a long time."

"Oh, in my case, you know," said the old man, "no one notices particularly whether I'm here or there."

"They don't?" I said.

At once he made a great effort to seem gay and said, as if to tease me, "Would you notice?"

But I was so much moved by an emotion I did not understand that I was unable to reply.

At that moment there was a surprising calm in the world around us. Even the lake was almost silent, as if it were the one now that was trying to hear what we had to say to each other. This caused us to lower our voices. Then we heard from somewhere far away, on the lake or in the woods around, the strange and frightening cry of a bird. But the old man loved this desolate cry.

"Hark! A loon!" he said. "I didn't think there'd be any left around here, for the loon is only happy in lonely places."

It seemed to please him that there was still at least one loon here. His old hand trailed in the sand. I looked at it for a moment without knowing I was looking at it, then I asked, "Is it bad to be old?"

He made a pretense of laughing at me but hid his hand behind his back.

"Whatever made you think such a thing?" he asked, and added, which seemed only to increase the mystery, "It's not so much worse to be old than it is to be young, you know. Look at all the little fusses you make for yourself!" But a few minutes later he sighed. "Still, it's always rather solemn beside the water when evening comes."

"Why is it solemn?" I asked.

He was beginning to look very tired again.

"All I know is that water seems to know more about

such things than the earth, perhaps because it is more ancient. Everything in creation began with water."

"Ah, everything began with water? You know so many things," I said almost enviously.

"And you as you grow older will know even more," he said.

But I did not wish to grow old. I wished to know everything without growing old; but above all, I imagine, I did not wish to see others grow old around me. Our newspaper hats lay beside us where we had abandoned them, trampled by people's feet. I tried to smooth mine out, wishing perhaps to take it with me as a souvenir. Suddenly I had tears in my eyes.

Alarmed, the old man put his hand under my chin and raised it so he could look into my face.

"What is it then? Are you bored all alone with an old man?"

"It's not that . . . it's not that. . . ."

"Well then, what?"

How could I make him understand about the weight of grief that had come to me, now that the brilliant color of things was extinguished, at seeing them look so dull and as if forsaken? And above all at having come so close finally to understanding the truth about old age and what it leads to? I looked at him with desolate eyes.

"But what is in the little head?" he asked. "Do you regret coming to see the lake?"

"Oh no. Oh no," I cried in a strange bewilderment, as if he had asked me: Do you regret being alive and having a heart, an imagination, parents, and me, your old friend? For though the lake—whose little phrase was still unintelligible— as it grew sad in the evening had saddened me as well, how could I blame it, any more than we can blame life for making us grow up in spite of ourselves?

"But what is it then?" the old man repeated.

And at last I unburdened myself to him.

"When one is very old," I asked, "does one have to die?"

"Ah!" he said. "So that's what's bothering you!"

I waited for his answer. No one had given me a proper answer to this. Perhaps he would. . . .

He passed his hand gently over my forehead.

"In the first place, there are birds that die young. . . ."

"Yes, that's true. I found one once."

"And," he continued, "it's sad to die young. Because one hasn't had time to learn and love enough. . . . Do you understand? But when one is old, it's natural."

"Natural?"

"The most natural thing there is. One has had one's life. One has a sort of inclination now to go and see what it's like on the other side."

"Ah! Because you've learned and loved enough on this side?"

He let his eyes stray for a long time over the lake, the sand, and the sky.

"Learned enough . . . loved enough . . . I don't know. Perhaps one has never learned and loved enough. I would like just a little more time. I suppose one would always like just a little more time."

I was slightly cheered, however, and I began once more to pile the sand in little mountains.

"The other side, the place you go when you're finished here, where is it?"

He smiled faintly as he considered my face, which was raised to him.

"If one knew exactly, it might seem less beautiful, less attractive. When you set out on your discoveries, isn't it pleasant not to know too precisely what it is you'll discover?"

"Because it's a discovery?"

"Yes," he said. "Quite so. A sort of discovery."

I was beginning to be deeply interested in this mysterious country that he was telling me about under the leaden sky.

"Will it be even more beautiful than beside the lake?"

"Probably. I have a sort of idea that one finds the people and things one has loved all together there."

"Then you may find my grandmother," I began quite gaily, then plunged back into the sadness from which he'd succeeded so well in drawing me.

I took a little scrap of wood from the beach beside me and began to trace marks in the sand. Then, as so many children like to do, as if to testify to their lives that, even though short, are already so full, I wrote my name in the sand and after it the figure eight.

"That's a good age," said the old man as he watched me. "It's the beginning."

But I seemed to hear in his voice a suggestion that he thought me lucky to be only at the beginning and this flung me back into my confused distress. I suppose I could not bear the joy of being at the beginning while he was at the end.

"My grandmother was very, very old when she died," I told him. "She was eighty."

"That's not as old as all that," said the old man.

"No?" I asked incredulously, and then, a terrible suspicion coming to me, I questioned him with my eyes.

"I'm a fair amount older than that myself," he said, hanging his head, as if he were a little ashamed of being so old. "Write it in the sand," he suggested.

He whispered in my ear. I wrote what he had whispered: eighty-four. God knows why I had the idea of setting down the figures, his age and my own, as a sum in arithmetic and subtracting one from the other. I was stricken by what remained to me and seemed to separate us from each other by a stretch of time even more mysterious than the extent of water and earth.

"Seventy-six years—that's a lot," I said.

He had studied my figuring in the sand and now he said, as if rejoicing for me, "It's curious. One says of someone who has arrived at an advanced age, as I have, that he has attained a good age. But you're the one who is at a good age. All that lovely long life ahead of you! What are you going to do with it?" he asked me as if in a game of riddles.

How could I know? Besides, I was rather disheartened, I think, by a sense of the inequality and injustice of life. Why, I wondered, did we not all reach the same age at the same time.

"It would be dull," he pointed out, "all the old folks together—or only the young."

"Yes," I agreed, "it would be dull."

Then he drew my attention to this. "It will give you all the time you need to see and discover."

And when I still did not stir, lost in my strange calculations of ages and years, he suggested, "The ocean, for instance. Don't you want to go and see the ocean?"

I became interested again then, as if in spite of myself.

"Certainly I'll go and see the ocean. Is it even more beautiful?"

"More beautiful! . . . More beautiful! . . . No, not necessarily. Only more vast. And after a certain degree of vastness . . ."

I interrupted him to repeat after him and savor this beautiful word, vastness, that I was hearing for the first time.

The old man, who liked to see me learn his words, gave me all the time I needed to put this one well into my head before he continued, "After a certain degree of breadth and vastness, the human eye can no longer distinguish the difference.

So we might very well be sitting beside the ocean at this moment."

"Oh yes!" I said, carried away into happiness in spite of myself. "Which, though? The Pacific Ocean? Or the Atlantic?"

"Why not both?" he said. "Since fundamentally they are of the same nature."

"Oh indeed? I didn't know."

"Next," said the old man, "there will be the Rocky Mountains. Don't you feel the desire to go to see them in real earnest?"

"Certainly I'll go in real earnest."

"And the great cities of the world? Do you not feel that you will be tempted someday to go and visit the great cities of the world?"

"Yes," I agreed. "I shall be tempted to visit the great cities of the world." And I asked him, "Have you yourself seen many of the great cities of the world—in real earnest?"

He gazed far across the lake, as if the lovely cities were perhaps there under the water, and said, a little sadly, "I've seen my share of them. I've seen Paris, London, Amsterdam . . . and then there's a most charming little city, Bruges."

"Would you like to be there again?"

"In Bruges, perhaps."

"And you won't go back?"

He seemed to rouse himself from a dream and said, "No, I think not. My travels have been made."

But now he had raised me to a pitch of enthusiasm and I was thinking of my own voyages that were still to be made.

"Someday I'll go and see what Bruges is like."

"Oh you will like it very much," the old man promised. "And when you're there, will you think for a moment that it was I who sent you to see Bruges?"

"Oh yes," I promised gaily. "I'll think of it," but I was saddened now by the thought of all the years I would have to wait before I could go to Bruges.

"Poor child," said the old man, placing his hand on my head. "You'd like to be everywhere already. You would put the clock forward if it were possible. I would set it back. Do you know that we make a funny pair?"

It didn't seem to me that we made a funny pair. We made the best possible pair, that was all. Yet it was at this moment perhaps that I realized most clearly that it couldn't last. I began again to study the old man's features anxiously.

To distract me, then, he began to tell me a sort of marvelous story that at the time I thought he was inventing.

"For when you have been everywhere," he said, "when you have visited the cities and the monuments, the museums and the palaces, when you have seen the oceans and the mountains, do you know that then you'll want something even better?"

"Ah yes?"

"Yes, the heart is made in such a way that the more it has the more it needs. You will realize then that you are only on the threshold of the true discovery, the great discovery."

I ceased piling up the sand in order to look at him attentively.

"Then what is the great discovery?" I asked.

As if it too were a country to be explored, he told me that everything shone with a special light there, that even ordinary humble things were illuminated by this light. Because, a single human being having been given to us, it was as if henceforth we possessed the earth.

It seemed to me that he was speaking of the two of us. But no, he said, this was an entirely different sort of thing. For the country of love was the most vast and profound there was, leading us from one point to another so far away from it that we could no longer even remember the point of departure.

This country seemed more and more attractive to me.

"I'll go there too," I said. "I'll go and I'll stay. I'll travel all over that beautiful country."

He considered me long and curiously then, as if seeing into the distance—and why should he not have seen into the distance, since to me he had always seemed to know everything?

"Yes," he said, "I think you will indeed know that country well."

Why did he look so weary then and as if fearful of something that might happen to me there? I should myself have liked to hear about that magic country all day and all night and all another day again. But he was silent now, too tired to continue.

In this way then, he had almost managed to distract me from the pain he had caused me by being so old. Only almost, for as soon as he was silent, I heard the lake's little phrase again, and it seemed to me plaintive and gentle. The sky had grown even darker. Was it possible that we would finally have rain? Maman would be glad of it for her flowers. Maman, Maman. My heart too full of emotion, I thought of her as of my one and final refuge. For these large things I had learned today exhausted me suddenly and made me wish to be no more than a little child. But would this ever be possible again? I seemed to have passed a frontier today, an actual boundary, and to have gone farther than I should. And the lake's little phrase still haunted me. "Good-by, good-by, my children," it said perhaps. Who knows? It had seemed to me that its words changed as my own feelings changed. But had they not changed because of the lake?

"Suppose we sleep a little," said the old man. "There's nothing more for us to do and we must restore our strength for the trip back. Your mother won't be pleased if you come home all worn out. Perhaps she'll say it's my fault."

"It's not your fault."

"Yes, it may be a little. However, we came only to refresh ourselves."

"To re-fresh our-selves," I said, yawning with fatigue.

"Come close to me," he said. "Put your head on my shoulder. You'll be warmer."

I did as he said and yawned again. The little phrase of the lake seemed to come from farther away and to lose itself in the wind that rose and surrounded us.

"On that other side where you said people go," I asked, half asleep, "will the lake be there too?"

"Perhaps . . . I daresay . . ." said the old man drowsily.

"But you said the lake would remain for the eternity of time. . . ."

"That's true. People pass, things remain. Would you want them to take away with them the things others need to have so they can go on living?"

I noticed a rather large, somber cloud dive toward us. Another gust of wind passed, throwing sand in our faces and carrying off our paper hats before I could catch them.

"Would you prefer to take shelter?" the old man asked me.

"No, let's stay."

"Very well then, we'll stay."

For a moment longer I struggled to make out what the lake was shouting now that it had begun to be choppy. But everything seemed to merge in a beautiful tumult of air and water, as the light of day still diminished. How strange is this universe where we must live, little creatures haunted by too many unknown things. After troubling us all day long and making us ask ourselves a thousand questions, now with its noise of water and wind, monotonous in the end, it pushed us gently toward sleep. Alone now on this long beach before immensity, we slept shoulder to shoulder.

When the old man wakened, it was almost night. He shook me anxiously. I could hear him saying as if from far away, "Heavens, what if we miss the train? What will your mother say?"

I heard, "Your mother, your mother, the train, the train," and did not know where I was, who was speaking to me, or what was this great noise of furious water in my ears. As I roused, I was amazed to find myself lying on the sand near a dark mass that heaved and growled dully only a few paces away. Then when memory returned, I thought I had had all possible happiness today since, having seen Lake Winnipeg languidly sleeping, I was now going to see it rising in a tempest. Abrupt choppy waves collided and slapped. But there was scarcely any light left and, beyond a short distance, I could distinguish only a dark seething, sprinkled with brief white sparks. I strained my eyes, trying to pierce the shadows and discover if over there, in the distance, there were not some little lake gulls letting themselves be rocked on the angry waves, delighted with the stormy weather.

But the old man was urging me. "Come along. Have you got your little purse? All your things? Don't forget anything but do come quickly. Have you thought what a state your mother will be in if we don't come back on the evening train? . . . Your poor, poor mother! . . ."

As he dragged me over the sand, both of us stumbling, and repeated constantly, "Your poor, poor mother," the words began to twist my heart. The wind whistled, the sand yielded under our steps, the waves lamented, and "Your poor, poor mother" seemed to become mingled in all this like a vague and terrible reproach. I knew then, I suppose, that she was indeed poor, she who had never seen Lake Winnipeg or the ocean or the Rocky Mountains, which she had so longed to see, speaking of them to us so much that she had driven us to abandon her, if need be, to traverse the world. I think I also understood to some slight extent that it is not enough to have a passion to go away to be able to go away, that even with this passion in one's heart one may remain a prisoner all one's life on a little street.

From then on it was I who directed the steps of the poor old man, pulling him by the hand and urging him on with cries of "Quick, quick, trains don't wait."

We slept briefly again on the train. What would there have been to see, in any event? Only the shadows of the scrubby trees of the savanna on the windowpanes, as I noticed vaguely once or twice when I half opened my eyes. Only the coils of smoke from the train tracing against the glass what looked like elderly faces creased with years and anguish. That is perhaps all I have actually retained from our journey home. But children register things so strangely, sometimes an entire day down to the slightest detail and then letting a great fragment of time slip away from them completely. Yet from the dark and impenetrable oblivion into which it has fallen, at times a sort of glow arises.

At last we were on the streetcar, both of us so worn out that we had not even strength to talk. Our heads swayed one against the other. But not long before we were to get off, the old man noticed that my hair ribbon had come undone and was hanging to one side. He tried to tie the bow again but his hands trembled. And besides, he told me, it was such a long time since he had tied a hair ribbon for a little girl.

We got out at our stop and the old man took my hand to escort me to my door. Because he was dragging his feet, I suggested that we part and each go his separate way home. I would only have a short stretch of fairly well-lighted street to traverse alone. But the old man was offended at the mere thought.

"Abandon a little lady in the middle of the street! Come along!"

At least, that, I believe, is what he said, for the old man was speaking so indistinctly now that I couldn't be sure. Or was it that I had become a little deaf from the murmuring of water that still sounded in my ears? I spoke of this to the old man, who told me it was always like this when one returned from a day spent beside a great expanse of water, that one continued to hear it like a humming, sometimes for two or three days.

But though we had brought the sound of the water back with us, we hadn't kept even a trace of its gentle coolness. We were already covered in perspiration.

"We've plunged right back into our steam bath," said the old man. "It's most peculiar. The air here hasn't even changed. One might think . . . one might think that what we've seen today is only a dream—nothing but a dream."

I could see all around us, in the glow from the street lamps, the poor leaves so heavy and weary from the heat. I heard our steps scraping against the pavement. The old man stumbled. I steadied him as best I could, but I had scarcely helped him right himself than I stumbled in my turn. The old man put out a hand to keep me from falling and tried to laugh, saying once again that we made a funny pair, that it was rather a case of the blind leading the blind. But his denture slipped down in his mouth and I had trouble understanding this business about the blind.

At last we were in front of the railing to which he must conduct me, he had said, since it was where he had met me that morning. Shaky on his feet as he was, he took time to remove his Caribbee hat in salutation, standing there all alone in the shadows. I remember how attractively the white splotch of his hat stood out against the hot night. I held him for a moment by the sleeve. I suppose I could not bear to see this day come to an end and disappear like others into that sort of finality that midnight represents. It seemed to me also that I still had one last important question to ask him, which had to do with what passes and what remains . . . and in which the loon with its solitary ways was in some inexplicable way mingled.

But then Maman came out of the house and ran toward us, crying, "Here they are, here they are!"

She looked at us both with the same expression, pity perhaps, and also a sort of avidity. Then the splendor and the strange sadness of all I had seen today came to me, like an imperishable song that I would never perhaps cease to hear a little. I threw myself into Maman's arms. I was almost weeping.

"I've seen it, I've seen it, Maman!" I cried. "Beautiful Lake Winnipeg!"

The Move

I HAVE perhaps never envied anyone as much as a girl I knew when I was about eleven years old and of whom today I remember not much more than the name, Florence. Her father was a mover. I don't think this was his trade. He was a handyman, I imagine, engaging in various odd jobs; at the time of the seasonal movings—and it seems to me that people changed their lodgings often in those days—he moved the household effects of people of small means who lived near us and even quite far away, in the suburbs and distant quarters of Winnipeg. No doubt, his huge cart and his horses, which he had not wanted to dispose of when he came from the country to the city, had made him a mover.

On Saturdays Florence accompanied her father on his journeys, which, because of the slow pace of the horses, often took the entire day. I envied her to the point of having no more than one fixed idea: Why was my father not also a mover? What finer trade could one practice?

I don't know what moving signified to me in those days. Certainly I could not have had any clear idea what it was like. I had been born and had grown up in the fine, comfortable house in which we were still living and which, in all probability, we would never leave. Such fixity seemed frightfully monotonous to me that summer. Actually we were never really away from that large house. If we were going to the country for a while, even if we were only to be absent for a day, the problem immediately arose: Yes, but who will look after the house?

To take one's furniture and belongings, to abandon a place, close a door behind one forever, say good-by to a neighborhood, this was an adventure of which I knew nothing; and it was probably the sheer force of my efforts to picture it to myself that made it seem so daring, heroic, and exalted in my eyes.

"Aren't we ever going to move?" I used to ask Maman.

"I certainly hope not," she would say. "By the grace of God and the long patience of your father, we are solidly established at last. I only hope it is forever."

She told me that to her no sight in the world could be more heartbreaking, more poignant even, than a house moving.

"For a while," she said, "it's as if you were related to the nomads, those poor souls who slip along the surface of existence, putting their roots down nowhere. You no longer have a roof over your head. Yes indeed, for a few hours at least, it's as if you were drifting on the stream of life."

Poor Mother! Her objections and comparisons only strengthened my strange hankering. To drift on the stream of life! To be like the nomads! To wander through the world! There was nothing in any of this that did not seem to me complete felicity.

Since I myself could not move, I wished to be present at someone else's moving and see what it was all about. Summer came. My unreasonable desire grew. Even now I cannot speak of it lightly, much less so with derision. Certain of our desires, as if they knew about us before we do ourselves, do not deserve to be mocked.

Each Saturday morning I used to go and wander around Florence's house. Her father—a big dirty-blond man in blue work clothes, always grumbling a little or even, perhaps, swearing—would be busy getting the impressive cart out of the barn. When the horses were harnessed and provided with nose bags of oats, the father and his little daughter would climb onto the high seat; the father would take the reins in his hands; they would both, it seemed to me, look at me then with slight pity, a vague commiseration. I would feel forsaken, of an inferior species of humans unworthy of high adventure.

The father would shout something to the horses. The cart would shake. I would watch them set out in that cool little morning haze that seems to promise such delightful emotions to come. I would wave my hand at them, even though they never looked back at me. "Have a good trip," I would call. I would feel so unhappy at being left behind that I would nurse my regret all day and with it an aching curiosity. What would they see today? Where were they at this moment? What was offering itself to their travelers' eyes? It was no use my knowing that they could go only a limited distance in any event. I would imagine the two of them seeing things that no one else in the world could see. From the top of the cart, I thought, how transformed the world must appear.

At last my desire to go with them was so strong and so constant that I decided to ask my mother for permission—although I was almost certain I would never obtain it. She held my new friends in rather poor esteem and, though she tolerated my hanging continually about them, smelling their

odor of horses, adventure, and dust, I knew in my heart of
hearts that the mere idea that I might wish to accompany
them would fill her with indignation.

At my first words, indeed, she silenced me.

"Are you mad? To wander about the city in a moving
wagon! Just picture yourself," she said, "in the midst of
furniture and boxes and piled-up mattresses all day, and with
who knows what people! What can you imagine would be
pleasant about that?"

How strange it was. Even the idea, for instance, of being
surrounded by heaped-up chairs, chests with empty drawers,
unhooked pictures—the very novelty of all this stimulated my
desire.

"Never speak of that whim to me again," said my mother.
"The answer is no and no it will remain."

Next day I went over to see Florence, to feed my nostalgic
envy of their existence on the few words she might say to me.

"Where did you go yesterday? Who did you move?"

"Oh I'm not sure," Florence said, chewing gum—she was
always either chewing gum or sucking a candy. "We went over
to Fort Rouge, I think, to get some folks and move them way
to hell and gone over by East Kildonan."

These were the names of quite ordinary suburbs. Why was
it that at moments such as these they seemed to hold the
slightly poignant attraction of those parts of the world that
are remote, mysterious, and difficult to reach?

"What did you see?" I asked.

Florence shifted her gum from one cheek to the other,
looking at me with slightly foolish eyes. She was not an im-
aginative child. No doubt, to her and her father the latter's
work seemed banal, dirty, and tiring, and nothing more similar to one household move than another household move.
Later I discovered that if Florence accompanied her father

every Saturday, it was only because her mother went out
cleaning that day and there was no one to look after the
little girl at home. So her father took her along.

Both father and daughter began to consider me a trifle
mad to endow their life with so much glamour.

I had asked the big pale-blond man countless times if he
wouldn't take me too. He always looked at me for a moment
as at some sort of curiosity—a child who perhaps wasn't completely normal—and said, "If your mother gives you permission . . ." and spat on the ground, hitched up his huge trousers with a movement of his hips, then went off to feed his
horses or grease the wheels of his cart.

The end of the moving season was approaching. In the
blazing heat of summer no one moved except people who
were being evicted or who had to move closer to a new job,
rare cases. If I don't soon manage to see what moving is
like, I thought, I'll have to wait till next summer. And who
knows? Next summer I may no longer have such a taste
for it.

The notion that my desire might not always mean so much
to me, instead of cheering me, filled me with anxiety. I began to realize that even our desires are not eternally faithful
to us, that they wear out, perhaps die, or are replaced by
others, and this precariousness of their lives made them
seem more touching to me, more friendly. I thought that if
we do not satisfy them they must go away somewhere and
perish of boredom and lassitude.

Observing that I was still taken up with my "whim,"
Maman perhaps thought she might distract me from it by
telling me once more the charming stories of her own childhood. She chose, oddly enough, to tell me again about the
long journey of her family across the prairie by covered

wagon. The truth must have been that she herself relived this thrilling voyage into the unknown again and again and that, by recounting it to me, she perhaps drained away some of that heartbreaking nostalgia that our life deposits in us, whatever it may be.

So here she was telling me again how, crowded together in the wagon—for Grandmother had brought some of her furniture, her spinning wheel certainly, and innumerable bundles—pressed closely in together, they had journeyed across the immense country.

"The prairie at that time," she said, "seemed even more immense than it does today, for there were no villages to speak of along the trail and only a few houses. To see even one, away far off in the distance, was an adventure in itself."

"And what did you feel?" I asked her.

"I was attracted," Maman admitted, bowing her head slightly, as if there were something a bit wrong, or at least strange, about this. "Attracted by the space, the great bare sky, the way the tiniest tree was visible in this solitude for miles. I was very much attracted."

"So you were happy?"

"Happy? Yes, I think so. Happy without knowing why. Happy as you are, when you are young—or even not so young —simply because you are in motion, because life is changing and will continue to change and everything is being renewed. It's curious," she told me. "Such things must run in families, for I wonder whether there have ever been such born travelers as all of us."

And she promised me that later on I too would know what it is to set forth, to be always seeking from life a possible beginning over—and that perhaps I might even become weary of it.

That night the intensity of my desire wakened me from sleep. I imagined myself in my mother's place, a child lying, as she had described it, on the floor of the wagon, watching the prairie stars—the most luminous stars in either hemisphere, it is said—as they journeyed over her head.

That, I thought, I shall never know; it is a life that is gone beyond recall and lost—and the mere fact that there were ways of life that were over, extinct in the past, and that we could not recover them in our day, filled me with the same nostalgic longing for the lost years as I had felt for my own perishable desires. But, for lack of anything better, there was the possible journey with our neighbors.

I knew—I guessed, rather--that, though we owe obedience to our parents, we owe it also to certain of our desires, those that are strangest, piercing, and too vast.

I remained awake. Tomorrow—this very day, rather—was a Saturday, moving day. I had resolved to go with the Pichettes.

Dawn appeared. Had I ever really seen it until now? I noticed that before the sky becomes clean and shining, it takes on an indecisive color, like badly washed laundry.

Now, the desire that was pushing me so violently, to the point of revolt, had no longer anything happy or even tempting about it. It was more like an order. Anguish weighed upon my heart. I wasn't even free now to say to myself, "Sleep. Forget all that." I had to go.

Is it the same anguish that has wakened me so many times in my life, wakens me still at dawn with the awareness of an imminent departure, sad sometimes, sometimes joyful, but almost always toward an unknown destination? Is it always the same departure that is involved?

When I judged the morning to be sufficiently advanced, I got up and combed my hair. Curiously enough, for this trip in a cart, I chose to put on my prettiest dress. "Might as well be hung for a sheep as a lamb," I said to myself, and left the house without a sound.

I arrived soon at the mover's. He was yawning on the threshold of the barn, stretching his arms in the early sun. He considered me suspiciously.

"Have you got permission?"

I swallowed my saliva rapidly. I nodded.

A little later Florence appeared, looking bad-tempered and sleepy.

She hitched herself up onto the seat beside us.

"Giddup!" cried the man.

And we set out in that cool morning hour that had promised me the transformation of the world and everything in it—and undoubtedly of myself.

2

And at first the journey kept its promise. We were passing through a city of sonorous and empty streets, over which we rolled with a great noise. All the houses seemed to be still asleep, bathed in a curious and peaceful atmosphere of withdrawal. I had never seen our little town wearing this absent, gentle air of remoteness.

The great rising sun bleached and purified it, I felt. I seemed to be traveling through an absolutely unknown city, remote and still to be explored. And yet I was astonished to recognize, as if vaguely, buildings, church spires, and street crossings that I must have seen somewhere before. But how could this be, since I had this morning left the world I had known and was entering into a new one?

Soon streetcars and a few automobiles began to move about. The sight of them looming upon the horizon and coming toward us gave me a vivid sense of the shifting of epochs.

What had these streetcars and automobiles come to do in our time, which was that of the cart? I asked myself with pleasure. When we reached Winnipeg and became involved in already heavy traffic, my sense of strangeness was so great that I believed I must be dreaming and clapped my hands.

Even at that time a horse-drawn cart must have been rare in the center of the city. So, at our side, everything was moving quickly and easily. We, with our cumbrous and reflective gait, passed like a slow, majestic film. I am the past, I am times gone by, I said to myself with fervor.

People stopped to watch us pass. I looked at them in turn, as if from far away. What did we have in common with this modern, noisy, agitated city? Increasingly, high in the cart, I became a survivor from times past. I had to restrain myself from beginning to salute the crowds, the streets, and the city, as if they were lucky to see us sweeping by.

For I had a tendency to divide into two people, actor and witness. From time to time I was the crowd that watched the passage of this astonishing cart from the past. Then I was the personage who considered from on high these modern times at her feet.

Meanwhile the difficulty of driving his somewhat nervous horses through all this noise and traffic was making the mover, whom I would have expected to be calmer and more composed, increasingly edgy. He complained and even swore noisily at almost everything we encountered. This began to embarrass me. I felt that his bad temper was spoiling all the pleasure and the sense of gentle incongruity that the poor people of the present era might have obtained from our appearance in their midst. I should have very much liked to dis-

associate myself from him. But how could I, jammed in beside him as I was?

Finally, we took to small, quieter streets. I saw then that
we were going toward Fort Garry.

"Is that the way we're going?"

"Yes," replied Monsieur Pichette ungraciously. "That's the
way."

The heat was becoming overpowering. Without any shelter,
wedged between the big bulky man and Florence, who made
no effort to leave me a comfortable place, I was beginning to
suffer greatly. At last, after several hours, we were almost in
the country.

The houses were still ranked along narrow streets, but now
these were short and beyond them the prairie could be seen
like a great recumbent land—a land so widespread that doubtless one would never be able to see either its end or its beginning. My heart began once more to beat hard.

There begins the land of the prairies, I said to myself. There
begins the infinite prairie of Canada.

"Are we going to go onto the real prairie?" I asked. "Or
are we still really inside the city limits?"

"You are certainly the most inquisitive little girl I've ever
seen in my life," grumbled Monsieur Pichette, and he told me
nothing at all.

Now the roads were only of dirt, which the wind lifted in
dusty whirlwinds. The houses spaced themselves out, became
smaller and smaller. Finally they were no more than badly
constructed shacks, put together out of various odds and ends
—a bit of tin, a few planks, some painted, some raw—and they
all seemed to have been raised during the night only to be
demolished the next day. Yet, unfinished as they were, the
little houses still seemed old. Before one of them we stopped.

————

The people had begun to pile up their belongings, in the house or outside it, in cardboard cartons or merely thrown pell-mell into bedcovers with the corners knotted to form rough bundles. But they were not very far along, according to Monsieur Pichette, who flew into a rage the moment we arrived.

"I only charge five dollars to move people," he said, "and they aren't even ready when I get here."

We all began to transport the household effects from the shack to the cart. I joined in, carrying numerous small objects that fell to my hand—saucepans with unmatching covers, a pot, a chipped water jug. I was trying, I think, to distract myself, to keep, if at all possible, the little happiness I had left. For I was beginning to realize that the adventure was taking a sordid turn. In this poor, exhausted-looking woman with her hair plastered to her face, and in her husband—a man as lacking in amiability as Monsieur Pichette—I was discovering people who were doomed to a life of which I knew nothing, terribly gray and, it seemed to me, without exit. So I tried to help them as much as I could and took it upon myself to carry some rather large objects on my own. At last I was told to sit still because I was getting in everyone's way.

I went to rejoin Florence, who was sitting a short distance away on a little wooden fence.

"Is it always like this?" I asked.

"Yes, like this—or worse."

"It's possible to be worse?"

"Much worse. These people," she said, "have beds, and dressers. . . . "

She refused to enlighten me further.

"I'm hungry," she decided and she ran to unpack a little lunch box, took out some bread and butter and an apple and proceeded to eat under my nose.

"Didn't you bring anything to eat?" she asked.

"No."

"You should have," she said, and continued to bite hungrily into her bread, without offering me a scrap.

I watched the men bring out some soiled mattresses, which they carried at arm's length. New mattresses are not too distressing a sight; but once they have become the slightest bit worn or dirty I doubt that any household object is more repugnant. Then the men carried out an old torn sofa on their shoulders, some bedposts and springs. I tried to whip up my enthusiasm, to revive a few flames of it, at least. And it was then, I think, that I had a consoling idea: we had come to remove these people from this wretched life; we were going to take them now to something better; we were going to find them a fine, clean house.

A little dog circled around us, whimpering, starving, perhaps anxious. For his sake more than my own maybe, I would have liked to obtain a few bits of Florence's lunch.

"Won't you give him a little bit?" I asked.

Florence hastily devoured a large mouthful.

"Let him try and get it," she said.

The cart was full now and, on the ground beside it, almost as many old things still waited to be stowed away.

I began to suffer for the horses, which would have all this to pull.

The house was completely emptied, except for bits of broken dishes and some absolutely worthless rags. The woman was the last to come out. This was the moment I had imagined as dramatic, almost historic, undoubtedly marked by some memorable gesture or word. But this poor creature, so weary and dust-covered, had apparently no regret at crossing her threshold, at leaving behind her two, three, or perhaps four years of her life.

"Come, we'll have to hurry," she said simply, "if we want to be in our new place before night."

She climbed onto the seat of the cart with one of the younger children, whom she took on her knees. The others went off with their father, to go a little way on foot, then by streetcar, to be ahead of us, they said, at the place where we were going.

Florence and I had to stand among the furniture piled up behind.

The enormous cart now looked like some sort of monster, with tubs and pails bouncing about on both sides, upturned chairs, huge clumsy packages bulging in all directions.

The horses pulled vigorously. We set out. Then the little dog began to run along behind us, whimpering so loudly in fear and despair that I cried, imagining that no one had thought of him, "We've forgotten the little dog. Stop. Wait for the little dog."

In the face of everyone's indifference, I asked the woman, whose name was Mrs. Smith, "Isn't he yours?"

"Yes, he's ours, I suppose," she replied.

"He's coming. Wait for him," I begged.

"Don't you think we're loaded up enough already?" the mover snapped dryly, and he whipped his horses.

For a long moment more the little dog ran along behind us.

He wasn't made for running, this little dog. His legs were too short and bowed. But he did his best. Ah yes! He did his best.

Is he going to try to follow us across the whole city? I thought with distress. Awkward, distracted, and upset as he was, he would surely be crushed by an automobile or a street-car. I don't know which I dreaded most: to see him turn back alone toward the deserted house or try to cross the city, come what might. We were already turning onto a street that was furrowed with tracks. A streetcar was approaching in the distance; several cars passed us, honking.

Mrs. Smith leaned down from the seat of the cart and shouted at the little dog, "Go on home."

Then she repeated, more loudly, "Go on home, stupid."

So he had a sort of name, even though cruel, yet he was being abandoned.

Overcome with astonishment, the little dog stopped, hesitated a moment, then lay down on the ground, his eyes turned toward us, watching us disappear and whimpering with fright on the edge of the big city.

And a little later I was pleased, as you will understand, that I did not need to look at him any longer.

3

I have always thought that the human heart is a little like the ocean, subject to tides, that joy rises in it in a steady flow, singing of waves, good fortune, and bliss; but afterward, when the high sea withdraws, it leaves an utter desolation in our sight. So it was with me that day.

We had gone back across almost the whole enormous city—less enormous perhaps than scattered, strangely, widely spread out. The eagerness of the day diminished. I even think the sun was about to disappear. Our monster cart plunged, like some worn-out beast, toward the inconvenient, rambling neighborhoods that lay at the exact opposite end of the city to the one from which we had come.

Florence was whiling away the time by opening the drawers of an old chest and thrusting her hand into the muddle inside —the exact embodiment, it seemed to me, of this day—bits of faded ribbon; old postcards on whose backs someone had one day written: Splendid weather, Best love and kisses; a quill from a hat; electricity bills; gas reminders; a small child's shoe. The disagreeable little girl gathered up handfuls of these things, examined them, read, laughed. At one point, sensing my disapproval, she looked up, saw me watching her rummage, and thumbed her nose in spite.

The day declined further. Once more we were in sad little streets, without trees, so much like the one from which we had taken the Smiths that it seemed to me we had made all this journey for nothing and were going to end up finally at the same shack from which I had hoped to remove them.

At the end of each of these little streets the infinite prairie once more appeared but now almost dark, barely tinted, on the rim of the horizon, with angry red—the pensive, melancholy prairie of my childhood.

At last we had arrived.

Against that red horizon a small lonely house stood out black, quite far from its neighbors—a small house without foundations, set upon the ground. It did not seem old but it was already full of the odor and, no doubt, the rags and tatters of the people who had left it a short time ago. However, they had not left a single light bulb in place.

In the semidarkness Mrs. Smith began to search through her bundles, lamenting that she was sure she had tucked two or three carefully away but no longer remembered where. Her husband, who had arrived a short time before us, distressed by the dimness and the clumsiness of his wife, began to accuse her of carelessness. The children were hungry; they started to cry with fretful frightened voices, in an importunate tone that reminded me of the whimpering of the little dog. The parents distributed a few slaps, a little haphazardly, it seemed to me. Finally Mrs. Smith found a light bulb. A small glow shone forth timidly, as if ashamed at having to illuminate such a sad beginning.

One of the children, tortured by some strange preference, began to implore, "Let's go home. This isn't our home. Oh let's go back home!"

Mrs. Smith had come across a sack of flour, a frying pan and some eggs while she was searching for light bulbs and now she courageously set to work preparing a meal for her family. It was this, I think, that saddened me most: this poor woman, in the midst of complete disorder and almost in the dark, beginning to make pancakes. She offered some to me. I ate a little, for I was very hungry. At that moment I believe she was sorry she had abandoned the little dog. This was the one small break in the terrible ending of this day.

Meanwhile Monsieur Pichette, in a grumbling anxiety to be finished, had completely emptied the cart. As soon as everything was dumped on the ground in front of the door, he came and said to Mr. Smith, "That's five dollars."

"But you have to help me carry it all in," said Mr. Smith.

"Not on your life. I've done all I have to."

Poor Mr. Smith fumbled in his pocket and took out five dollars in bills and small change, which he handed to the mover.

The latter counted the money in the weak glimmer that came from the house and said, "That's it. We're quits."

In this glimmer from the house I noticed that our poor horses were also very tired. They blinked their eyes with a lost expression, the result of too many house movings, no doubt. Perhaps horses would prefer to make the same trip over and over again—in this way they would not feel too estranged from their customary ways. But, always setting out on new routes, toward an unknown destination, they must feel disconcerted and dejected. I had time, by hurrying, to fetch them each a handful of tender grass at the end of the street where the prairie began.

What would we have had to say to each other on our way back? Nothing, certainly, and so we said nothing. Night had fallen, black, sad, and impenetrable, when we finally reached the old stable, which had once seemed to me to contain more magic and charm than even the cave of Aladdin.

The mover nevertheless reached out his hand to help me down from the cart. He was one of those people—at least I thought so then—who, after being surly and detestable all day, try at the last moment to make amends with a pleasant word for the bad impression they have created. But it was too late, much too late.

"You're not too tired?" he asked, I believe.

I shook my head and after a quick good night, an unwilling thank you, I fled. I ran toward my home, the sidewalk resounding in the silence under my steps.

I don't believe I thought of rejoicing at what I was returning to—a life that, modest as it was, was still a thousand miles away from that of the Pichettes and the Smiths. And I had not yet realized that this whole shabby, dull, and pitiless side of life that the move had revealed to me today would further increase my frenzy to escape.

I was thinking only of my mother's anxiety, of my longing to find her again and be pardoned by her—and perhaps pardon her in turn for some great mysterious wrong whose point I did not understand.

She was in such a state of nervous tension, as a matter of fact—although neighbors had told her I had gone off early with the Pichettes—that when she saw me it was her exasperation that got the upper hand. She even raised her hand to strike me. I did not think of avoiding punishment. I may even have wanted it. But at that moment a surge of disillusion-

ment came over me—that terrible distress of the heart after
it has been inflated like a balloon.

I looked at my mother and cried, "Oh why have you said
a hundred times that from the seat of the covered wagon on
the prairie in the old days the world seemed renewed, different, and so beautiful?"

She looked at me in astonishment.

"Ah, so that's it!" she said.

And at once, to my profound surprise, she drew me toward
her and cradled me in her arms.

"You too then!" she said. "You too will have the family
disease, departure sickness. What a calamity!"

Then, hiding my face against her breast, she began to croon
me a sort of song, without melody and almost without words.

"Poor you," she intoned. "Ah, poor you! What is to become of you!"

The Road Past Altamont

ONE fine sunny day when we were driving, my mother and I, across the prairie in my little car and for hours had seen the vast, always flat horizons unwind before our slightly weary eyes, I heard Maman complain gently beside me, "Why is it, Christine, that in all this immense plain God never thought of putting at least a few hills?"

She had talked to us a great deal in the last years of the hills in the old province of Quebec where she was born: a severe little range with peaks and notches prolonged by spruce trees, an almost hostile troupe guarding the impoverished backway region. There was nothing in this, I felt, to be so much missed. Yet we were still deeply involved with this countryside that had been left behind at the beginning of our family, as if a mysterious and troubled relationship persisted between us and the abandoned hills that had never been quite settled. My own knowledge of it was slight: one day Grandfather saw in his imagination—because of the closed-in hills perhaps?—an immense open plain. At once he was ready to set out, for such was his nature. Grandmother, herself as stable as her hills, resisted for a long time. At last she was overcome. It is almost always, in a family, the dreamer that prevails. This then was what I understood about this matter of the lost hills.

And on this particular day again, not knowing that I was hurting Maman, I said, "Now come, Mother old dear. Your hills were just like all the other hills. It's only because your imagination has embroidered your childhood memories that they seem so attractive to you today. If you were to see them again, you'd be disappointed."

"Ah no," said Maman, who was always irritated when anyone tried to disparage the hills that had been lost to her sight for almost sixty years. And she firmly denied that her splendid imagination could have touched up the faded contours of such a faraway landscape.

And she began to tell me about it again as we crossed the flattest country in the world, the vast plain of southern Manitoba, which is so bare that a single lonely tree can be seen from a great distance and the least things appearing far away upon its surface take upon themselves a unique and pathetic value. Even the flight of a bird, suspended in so much space, twists the heart.

"Imagine," said Maman, "that everything was suddenly turned upside down. We'd see debris, a great mass of bare rocks, others thinly covered with moss. Next would come some low wooded hills, and the folds between them are the most curious thing in the world. One keeps going on, Christine, to discover what can be between them. But once again the escarpment opens out. One is compelled to explore another fold. One is always in suspense."

"Yes, perhaps," I said.

I myself passionately loved our open plains. I didn't think I would have the patience for those closed-in regions that keep drawing us forward by one trick after another. It was undoubtedly the prairie's lack of secretiveness that delighted me most, its lofty and open countenance—although, all of infinity reflected in its boundless extent, is it not itself the most secret country? I could not conceive of there being any hills between me and this reminder of the total enigma, nor any other fleeting accident against which my eye might strike. It seemed to me that this would have thwarted and diminished the vague but powerful summons toward a thousand possibilities that my being received from it.

"Ah, you don't understand," said Maman. "It's the unexpected height, when you attain it, that gives meaning to all the rest."

But she seemed to have forgotten her old longing, which had returned to her for an instant, so fresh and so piercing. It was September, one of those beautiful days that are still warm but to which the resigned, slightly grayish sky and the stripped earth give an indefinable and touching air of gentle sadness. These are the abandoned days, which belong neither to summer nor yet to winter, and my mother began to look eagerly about her. At heart she was still too much alive, too much in love with life, to prefer a time already fixed in her memory to one that was still on its way to lose itself there, like a tributary to the ocean. She agreed with me that the uniformly golden color of the cropped straw and the uniform blue-gray of the sky formed a grave and profound beauty, although too unvarying perhaps for the needs of the heart. But what fine weather for traveling, she said. Yes, autumn was admirably suited to journeys, to all journeys. . . .

Then, just when I thought she was over her regret, I heard her sigh, "But this lack of trees everywhere—trees and water. In my little hills, Christine, the elements are mixed, the aspens, the birches, the maples. . . . Oh our sugar maples that turned so red in the autumn . . . the beeches also flamed with color.

And below, flowing from cove to cove, capturing all the colors, was our little Assomption River."

I was astonished to see Maman pass over her adult existence in Manitoba to go to the most remote part of her life in search of those images, unknown to me yesterday and now seemingly more pleasing to her than any others. I was perhaps even somewhat vexed.

We arrived then at a crossroads, and I thought of something else; I reflected for a moment, or perhaps, on the contrary, did not reflect at all. Today again a sort of light mist seems to lie across that day and I am still unable to be quite clear about what happened to us when I reached that lonely branching of the roads.

2

Do you know the rectilinear and inflexible narrow roads that crisscross the Canadian prairie, making of it a huge chessboard, above which the pensive sky seems to have been deliberating for a long time over which piece it will move, if indeed it will move any. One can get lost there; one often does get lost. Before me, meeting and parting in the same instant, stretched flat upon the grass like the arms of a huge cross, were two little dirt roads, absolutely identical and without signposts, as taciturn as the sky and the silent prairie all around, which absorbed only the rustle of the grasses and, from time to time, the far-off trilling of an unseen bird.

I had completely forgotten the directions my uncle had given me when we set out: turn to the left, then to the right, then to the left. These roads, I assure you, form a sort of vast confusing game and, if one goes wrong a single time, the error will multiply itself to infinity. But perhaps this was precisely what I wanted. At this lonely crossroads I may have been bewitched to the point of not wishing to decide anything for myself, unknown roads having always drawn me as do certain anonymous faces glimpsed in the middle of a crowd. I committed myself, I think, to chance—and yet was it chance that brought such prodigious things to pass that day? I committed myself then to the one of the two roads that seemed to me the most completely strange. Yet actually both were equally strange. Can it be that one, similar as it was to the other, gave me a sort of intelligible signal?

We had not been driving for more than a quarter of an hour along this out-of-the-way road, always flat upon the fields, when it crossed another of its fellows, leading into the distance. Once again, it seemed to me, I refused to choose and let myself be guided by caprice or intuition, by whatever it is we prefer to rely upon at times rather than our own judgment alone.

Now we were lost, of that there could be no doubt. If I had decided to retrace my steps at that point, it is doubtful if I could have repeated a journey that had been guided so entirely by caprice. So I might as well continue to go on. This I did, quickened, I think, by a secret delight at finding ourselves lost on this immense prairie that had no hiding place at all.

These roads in the depths of rural Manitoba, which I had taken to save time, as a short cut to the highway, we call section roads, and there are no others like them for going farther and nowhere. Tedious roads that cut the back country into a thousand squares, in those faraway, unimaginably lonely places—I miss them still today. I see once more their silent meeting under that enigmatic sky; the wind, lightly playing with them, raises dust from their surfaces and makes it

turn in a lasso. I recall their soundless greeting, their astonishment at coming together and parting again so soon—and for
what destination? For of whence they have come and where
they are going they never say a word. When I was young, it
seemed to me that they existed for no practical purpose, but
only for the strange excitement the mind obtains from playing with them in childish and fascinating games.

So I drove on at random. It was quite necessary, anyway,
for who was there in this dead region from whom I could ask
the way? For more than an hour we had not seen even as
much as the roof of a barn lost in the distance. There were
not even any power lines across this wild country. I was
happy for the instant as I have rarely been in my life.

I have never been sure what the source of this happiness
was. No doubt it was a matter of confidence, unlimited confidence in a future that seemed itself to be unlimited. Whereas
my mother had to return to the past for her joys, mine were
all ahead, almost all of them intact—and is it not a marvelous
moment when everything life has to give can be seen intact
upon the horizon, through the charm and magic of the unknown?

Maman was half asleep. Her head nodded slightly. From
time to time she partly opened her eyes, undoubtedly struggling
against her tiredness with that fear I had known in her all her
life, the fear that if she rested for a minute or even dozed off, in
that precise instant she would miss the best and most interesting thing that could happen. The heat and the monotony
overcame her curiosity in spite of her. Her head fell forward
again, her eyelids beat heavily, and, as they slipped over her
eyes, I noticed in their expression a physical weariness so great
that soon perhaps all Maman's eagerness and love of life would
no longer be able to prevail against it. And I remember I said

to myself something like: I mustn't wait too long to give Maman happiness. She may not be able to wait for it much longer. At that time I imagined that it was on the whole rather easy to make someone happy, that a tender word, a caress, or a smile could be enough. I imagined that it was in our power to fulfill the deepest needs of the heart, not yet knowing that tragic desires for perfection haunt some people till the end or, on the other hand, desires of such purity and simplicity that even the best will in the world would not know how to satisfy them.

I was perhaps slightly annoyed with my mother for wishing something other than what I considered it right to wish for her. If the truth be told, I was astonished that, old and sometimes weary as she was, Maman still entertained desires that seemed to me to be those of youth. I said to myself: Either one is young and it is time to strike out to know the world or one is old and it is time to rest and give up.

So a hundred times a day I said to Maman, "Rest. Haven't you done enough? It's time for you to rest."

And, as if I had insulted her, she would reply, "Rest! Believe me, it will soon enough be time for that."

Then, becoming thoughtful, she would say, "You know, I spoke that way to my own mother when she seemed to me to be growing old. 'When are you ever going to give up and rest?' I used to say to her, and only now can I see how provoking it must have been."

Our quiet, haphazardly chosen road had seemed for some time to be climbing, without perceptible strain, by slight and very gentle slopes, no doubt. However, the motor was puffing a little, and, if this hadn't been enough to tell me, I would have realized from the drier, more invigorating air that we were gaining altitude, sensitive as I have always been to the slightest atmospheric variation. With closed eyes, I think, I would recognize from the first breath the air of the ocean, the air of the plain, and certainly that of the high plateaus, because of the delightful feeling of lightness it communicates to me, as if I shed weight as I climbed—or mistakes.

Then, as we continued to rise, I seemed to see, spread against the sky, a distant, half-transparent range of small blue hills.

I was accustomed to the mirages of the prairies and this was the time of day when they arose, extraordinary or completely reasonable—sometimes great stretches of shimmering water, heavy, lifeless lakes. Often the Dead Sea itself appeared among us, level with the horizon; at other times phantom villages around their grain elevators. And once in my childhood an entire city rose from the ground at the end of the prairie especially for me, a strange city with cupolas.

Those are only clouds, I told myself, nothing more—and yet I pressed on as if to reach those gentle little hills before they were effaced.

But they did not melt away, like an illusion, sooner or later. Time and again, when I had rested my glance elsewhere, I found them still there when I looked back. They seemed to sharpen, to increase in size, and even perhaps become more beautiful. Then—did I dream all this? In so many things in our life an element of the imprecise and inexplicable persists, which makes us doubt their reality—the prairie, which since the beginning of the ages had been level and submissive, appeared to revolt. First it exploded in swellings, in crevices, in eroded cracks; boulders broke the surface. Then it split more deeply; ridges sprang up, took on height and came rushing from every side as if, delivered from its heavy immobility, the land was beginning to move and was coming toward me in waves quite as much as I was going toward it. Finally, there was no more doubt possible. Little hills formed on either side of us; they accompanied us at a fixed distance, then suddenly drew near and now we were completely enclosed.

Now, moreover, the dirt road was perceptibly climbing, without pretense, with a sort of elation, in joyous little bounds, in leaps like a young dog straining at the leash, and I had to change gears in mid-hill. From time to time as we passed, a liquid voice, some flow of water over the rocks, struck my ear.

Ah, Maman is right, I thought. Hills are exciting, playing a game of waiting and withholding with us, keeping us always in suspense.

And soon, just as my mother had wished, they showed themselves to be covered with dry bushes, with small trees insecurely rooted on inclining slopes but warmed by the sun, shot with ardent light, the luminous tones of their foliage trembling in the sunlit air. All this—the patches of scorched rock, the red berries on their slender branches, the scarlet leaves of the underbrush—was delightfully tangled together, almost dead, and yet meanwhile what a shout of life it gave!

Then, abruptly, my mother woke up.

Had she been informed during her sleep that the hills had been found again? At any rate, when the landscape was at its most beautiful, she opened her eyes, just as I was about to pull her by the sleeve and say, "Look, just look what's happened to you, Mamatchka!"

At first she appeared to be sunk in a profound bewilderment. Did she believe she had been carried back to the land of her childhood, returned to her starting point with her whole long life to be lived over again? Or did it seem to her that the landscape was mocking at her desires, offering her only an illusion?

But I still didn't know her. Always prompter to faith and to reality than I was, Maman soon realized the simple, delightful truth.

"Can you believe it, Christine!" she cried. "We're in the Pembina Mountains. You know—the only range of mountains in southern Manitoba. I've always wanted to see them. Your uncle assured me there was no way in. But there is, there is, and you, dear child, have discovered it!"

How would I dare to touch her joy that day, much less try to take it apart to grasp its inmost spring? All joy is so mysterious that I am always most conscious in its presence of the clumsiness of words and of the impiety of wishing to be always analyzing, trying to take the human heart by surprise.

And then everything that took place between Maman and the little hills was so silent. I went slowly to let her look at them at her ease, watching the way her eyes flew from one side of the road to the other. We were still climbing, and the hills continued to hurry to the right, then to the left, as if to see us pass, since they in their isolation could not have seen human beings any oftener than we saw hills. Then I stopped; I turned off the engine. In her anxiety to get out, Maman no longer knew which handle to turn to open the door. I helped her. Then, without a word, she set out alone into the hills.

She began to climb, between the dry bushes that caught for an instant at her skirt, surprisingly agile, with the movements of a young goat, raising her head from time to time toward the height . . . then I lost sight of her. When she reappeared a short time later, she was right on top of one of the steepest hills, a silhouette diminished by the distance, completely alone on the farthermost point of the rock. Beside her leaned a small twisted fir tree, which had found its niche up there among the winds. And the curious thought came to me as I saw them there side by side, Maman and the tree, that it is perhaps necessary to be quite alone at times in order to find oneself.

What did they say to each other that day, Maman and the little hills? Did the hills really give Maman back her joyous childhood heart? And why is it that a human being knows no greater happiness in old age than to find in himself once more the face he wore as a child? Wouldn't this be rather an infinitely cruel thing? Whence comes the happiness of such an encounter? Perhaps, full of pity for the vanished youthful soul, the aged soul calls to it tenderly across the years, like an echo. "See," it says, "I can still feel what you felt . . . love what you loved. . . ." And the echo undoubtedly answers something . . . but what? I knew nothing of this dialogue at that time. I merely wondered what could hold my mother for so long, in the open wind, on the rock. And if it was her past life she was finding there, how could there be happiness in this? How could it be good at seventy to give one's hand to one's childhood on a little hill? And if this is what life is, to find one's childhood again, at that moment then, when in their own good time childhood and old age come together again, the round must be almost finished, the festival over. I was suddenly terribly eager to see Maman back with me once more.

At last she came down from the hill. To conceal her emotion, she plucked a branch of red glowing leaves from a half-dead bush and, as she came toward me, caressed her bowed cheek with this. For she kept her eyes hidden from me as she approached and did not reveal them to me till quite a long time later, when there was no longer anything but ordinary things between us.

She sat down beside me without saying a word. We drove on in silence. From time to time I looked at her stealthily; I saw joy sparkling in her eyes like far-off water and even, for an instant, break to the surface in real moisture. So what she had seen was so disturbing? I was anxious all at once. The hills seemed different now, humped and rather cheerless; I longed to find the frank clear plain again.

Then Maman seized my arm in agitation.

"Christine," she asked, "did you just find this marvelous road by mistake?"

"So the thoughtlessness of youth is good for something!" I said jokingly.

But I saw that she was really troubled.

"In fact," she said, "you may not be able to find it again when we're coming back from your uncle's next year. You may never be able to find it again. There are roads, Christine, that one loses forever."

"What would you have me do?" I teased her gently. "Scatter bread crumbs like Tom Thumb?"

At that moment the hills opened out a little and, lodged completely in a crevice between fir trees, a tiny settlement appeared, rather like a mountain village with its four or five houses clinging at different levels to the uneven ground. On one of them shone a red Post Office sign. We had scarcely glimpsed the poor hamlet before it was hidden from our sight, though the singing of a stream, somewhere on the rocks, followed us for a moment longer. Maman had had time to catch the name of the place from the Post Office sign, a name that had, I think, fixed itself like an arrow in her spirit.

"It's Altamont," she said, glowing.

"Well, there's your landmark," I said, "since you're determined to have something definite about the journey."

"Yes," she said, "and let's never forget it, Christine. Let's engrave it in our memories. It's our only key to these hills, all we know for certain, the Altamont road."

And as she was speaking, our hills abruptly subsided, dwindled into scarcely raised mounds of earth, and almost at once the prairie received us, stretching away on every side in its obliterating changelessness, denying everything that was not itself. With one accord Maman and I turned to look behind us. Of the hills that were already beginning to withdraw into the night almost nothing remained, only a faint contour against the sky, a barely perceptible line such as children make when they amuse themselves drawing the earth and the sky.

3

Once again, next year in the autumn, the season of harvesting that she loved so well, I set out with my mother for our annual visit to her brothers. There were always two periods in the year when my mother was absolutely unable to be still, when her spirit, which was always close to the seasons, received from them the most irresistible summons—when it was time to sow and when it was time to reap. She would be informed, it seems to me, in a mysterious way. In the middle of the city, walking along the sidewalk or perhaps in a store, Maman would sniff the air, raise her head, and announce, "Cléophas will have begun to plant his wheat today. . . ." She would endure two or three days of agitation and restlessness, undertaking at one and the same time her spring house cleaning, some dressmaking, trips into town, and countless other things, to trick her migratory instinct, no doubt—for if ever one of us was possessed by it, it was certainly she, before she realized that it would attack us all in turn, her children, and snatch us from her.

We arrived at Uncle Cléophas's house in the midst of the threshing.

What activity used to prevail at that season on our Manitoba farms! Twelve to fifteen men lodged at the farm, some of them in the big house, others sleeping in small sheds fitted out as dormitories, furnished with camp beds, and with sometimes, it seems to me, a window pierced in their sides, unless there was only a door left constantly open to admit air.

These people, at once hired men, guests, and friends—but how to define the excellent relations we had with each other? —came from every corner of Canada, I should perhaps say of the world, for that was the most astonishing thing of all, that men of such diverse nationalities and characters were gathered together in our remote farms to harvest the wheat. There were young students fresh from the university, whom we heard talking all day long about reforms and changes; old fellows without an illusion about anything; rovers and born storytellers who seemed to live only for the evenings, when they held the floor; immigrants of all sorts, of course; in short, sad people and roisterers, and all of them, no matter what they told us, told us a little of their lives.

As I think now of those evenings long ago at my uncle's, in his house in the middle of the night on the prairie, it seems to me that I have my ear pressed against one of those conch shells from which a tireless murmur is to be heard. In that out-of-the-way farmhouse something of the universe vibrated. For these men were never so tired that they did not attempt, when night came and the whining of the machines was silenced for a few hours, to share something unique to each of them that might draw them for a moment closer to each other.

It is from those evenings, unfolding like competitions of songs and stories, that my desire, which has never since left me, to learn to tell a story well undoubtedly dates, so much was I impressed at that time by the poignant and miraculous power of this gift.

Maman, it is true, had always given me an example of it,

but never so much so as at these times of powerful stimulation when the past lived again in her with particular force, for this farm of my uncle's, which was actually modern for the period, had come to him from Grandfather, who broke the virgin soil himself.

The old theme of my grandparents' arrival in the west had been to my mother a sort of canvas on which she had worked all her life as one works at a tapestry, tying threads and commenting upon events like fate, so that the story varied, enlarged, and became more complex as the narrator gained age and perspective. Now when my mother related it again, I could scarcely recognize the lovely story of times past that had so enchanted my childhood; the characters were the same, the route was the same, and yet nothing else was as it used to be.

Sometimes we interrupted her.

"But that detail didn't appear in your first versions. That detail is new," we said with a hint of resentment perhaps, so anxious were we, I imagine, that the past at least should remain immutable. For if it too began to change . . .

"But it changes precisely as we ourselves change," said Maman.

I had gone out that evening, I remember, to breathe the scented air for a few minutes. Two paces from the house, a sort of impenetrable night began, just as in the times so often described to us by Maman. I went down to the end of the farm road, to the edge of the immense plateau, so somber at that hour and rustling like a great cloak spread out in the wind. How easy it was, with the darkness blotting out all traces of habitation, to imagine these places in the primitive reverie that had so excited my grandfather but always rebuffed my grandmother. On those nights of mild and vaguely plaintive wind, I was always aware of those two profoundly divided spirits. And my own adventurous heart perhaps divided them even further by inclining me so strongly toward the one who had so loved adventure.

I retraced my steps and, before I could see the lights of the house at the end of the wood, I heard, from another direction, an indistinct, muffled, vaguely happy sound. It was the rumination of the big farm horses in the stable full of animals exhausted by the labors of the day—a slow weary rhythm that had in it also, I thought, something of the contentment of repose.

In the big living room, where a few of our people were lingering, I found my mother and Uncle Cléophas, sitting a little to one side and engaged at this very moment in calling to mind the character of my grandmother.

"Do you remember the sudden anger she turned on us, Eveline," said my uncle, "that first night on the wagon trail when we couldn't find a house to stop in and had to camp out under the stars? Was it because the fire wouldn't catch? Or in fear of the naked prairie all around? She stood up, calling us gypsies, and said threateningly, 'All right. I've had enough of following you, you band of strangers. You go your way then. I'll go mine.' "

Maman smiled rather sadly.

"Those are the sorts of threats one makes when one is at the end of one's tether. Before she left her village, she probably didn't realize how different everything would be. The night you speak of must have been when she finally saw all the implications."

"But to call us strangers!"

"Weren't we, in a sense," said Maman, "when we all turned against her to extract her consent by force?"

"We had to," my uncle insisted. "We had to leave. Back in the hills, you remember, Eveline, it was nothing but rocks, thin soil. . . ."

"No doubt," said Maman. "But she was attached to it, and you must know now yourself that one doesn't only become attached to what is soft and easy."

Hidden in a corner of the room, a very young man was softly playing a harmonica. The slightly languid air formed a discreet accompaniment to their speech and perhaps urged them a little toward nostalgia.

"What could we have done but what we did?" my uncle continued. "The west was calling us. It was the future then. Besides, it proved to be right."

"It was the future," said Maman. "Now it's our past. At least let's try, in the light of what we've learned by living, to understand what it was like for her to have to leave her past when she was no longer young. Would you, Cléophas, willingly leave this farm you've inherited?"

"That's not the same thing," said my uncle defensively. "I've worked so hard here."

Maman appeared to be listening to someone invisible, a soul that had vanished perhaps but had not yet stopped trying to make itself heard. She raised her eyes to her brother and gave him a smile of indulgent rebuke.

"Cléophas, haven't you ever understood how hard she had to work on that wretched farm in order to make a life for us that was pleasant on the whole?"

"That's true," said my uncle, somewhat ashamed. "But I was so young when we left the hills. I scarcely remember them. What about you? Do you remember?"

Maman stared dreamily at her clasped hands.

"I remember them, yes, quite well."

But what was she recalling exactly? The bygone hills she had not seen since childhood? Or the quite unexpected ones in Manitoba, which we had one day discovered, which had restored so much else to her memory and which must have been the source of the change I had observed in her, for, come to think of it, it was only since the reappearance of hills in our life that I had noticed that attention to voices from the past that I found so bewildering and that took her to some extent away from me.

Suddenly I had had enough of all this chiaroscuro. After all, since hills were in some way involved in all this, we might as well speak of them openly, settle the matter once for all. It occurred to me that she had not spoken of them to me even once in this whole year, although she thought of them incessantly, I was convinced.

I broached the subject.

"Uncle Cléophas," I said, "do you know the village of Altamont? Less than a village, actually—just a few houses . . ."

"Altamont!" my uncle repeated, tranquilly smoking his pipe. "Queer little spot, isn't it? It's been half dead for a long time. I've never liked that region. It's too cramped and narrow. I've never been able to understand why, with the choice of homesteads on the level easy prairie, anyone would look at that clump of hills. Yet it happened some fifty years ago. At least the region attracted some Scottish immigrants who, I imagine, found there a smaller edition of the country they had left. But what folly! The Highlanders didn't make a go of it and scattered after a short while, some returning home, others going to the towns. An experiment that turned into a disaster, that's Altamont."

"Nevertheless," I said, hearing myself speak on Maman's behalf, "there are some extraordinary views to be seen when you cross the entire little range."

"Do you say there's a road right across the range? If so, it must be in a bad state of repair, for almost no one, to my knowledge, ever goes there now."

I noticed then that Maman was watching me nervously, as if she feared I might let my uncle too far into our secrets, and with her eyes she cautioned me against it. Good and affable as he was, my uncle was not much given to flights of the imagination and knew how to squelch them sometimes with a single, too concrete word. It was curious: the true son, at heart, of my grandmother, the one most exactly like her, with his realistic spirit and his attachment to what he possessed, he was because of his lack of imagination the one least capable of understanding her. The conversation took another turn. A little old Norwegian, hired by my uncle, often close-mouthed and yet loquacious in his own good time, suddenly began in his strong rough accent to describe the mountains of his native land and the great fjords profoundly open to the sea.

On these evenings of memories and melancholy, many times we found thus, at dreamy distances, lost horizons.

4

The time came for us to be on our way. I sensed, without her saying a word, that Maman was preoccupied again by the thought of the hills, perhaps by the tender look on her face, that absently tender look a face wears when it is withdrawn from the present.

We set out in silence. After passing through a few villages, along still slightly traveled roads, we reached an almost un-inhabited prairie at the end of which a slight rise of land was outlined in faint relief.

And once again, by narrow taciturn roads, from crossing to silent crossing, without considering, without hesitation, as if the place to which I was going was not on the map but only somewhere at the limit of faith, between the sighing grasses and the dust rising in melancholy spirals on either side, proceeding as if in a dream from intersection to intersection, I drove my mother directly into the hills. But she did not waken to find them there complete, because she had been watching for them for some time, sitting on the edge of the seat, and saw them approach with a sort of peaceful joy that contrasted strongly with her agitation of the previous trip. But this happy reassurance, which came undoubtedly from the awareness that the hills were indeed real, was tinged with a tender melancholy, perhaps because, finding them so real, she would have to say to them as well a sort of good-by.

I don't know why I began to question her about Grandmother.

"Was she quarrelsome all her life?" I asked. "Or did that just come upon her later on?"

Maman seemed to rouse herself from a dream.

"It's curious that you should speak of her at the exact moment I was thinking how lonely she must have been among us, her husband and her children, who were all, you might say, of a different breed. I would have liked to call her back to earth, for a moment at least, and try to set things right with her."

"But Grandfather, with his dreams she didn't wish to share, must also have been lonely. . . ."

"Yes, undoubtedly . . . It's strange," she went on, "what takes place in us as we live, the way the beings who gave us life continue, in us and through us, to struggle against each other, each wishing to have us completely on his side."

"That's a rather frightening thing you're saying."

"Frightening? Why no, quite fair from their point of view, though for the one who has to suffer this division it isn't always easy."

Her eyes lit up slightly as she admitted, "When I was very young I recognized myself perfectly in my father. We were allies, he and I. Maman used to say of us, with some rancor perhaps, 'As thick as thieves.' I believed I took entirely after him and I think I was glad of it. . . . I loved him almost to the exclusion of everyone else."

"And then?"

"Later," said Maman, "with the first disillusionments of life, I began to detect in myself a few small signs of the personality of my mother. But I didn't want to resemble her, admirable as she was, poor old thing, and I fought against it. Only with middle age did I catch up with her, or she caught up with me —how can you explain this strange encounter outside time? One day, imagine my stupefaction, I caught myself making one of her gestures, which from the first time I made it came to me as naturally as breathing. Even my face began to change. When I was young, I was said to be the living image of your grandfather. Then little by little, from day to day, I saw my face alter as if as the result of an invisible, determined, and boundless will. And now can you honestly say that I don't bear an astonishing resemblance to that picture we have of Grandmother when she was just my present age?"

I gave her a troubled look and could not help admitting that there was something in what she said.

"In your face perhaps, but not in your character."

"In my character too, believe me. Besides, I'm no longer angry about it, since, having become her, I understand her. Ah, that is certainly one of life's most surprising experiences. We give birth in turn to the one who gave us birth when finally, sooner or later, we draw her into our self. From then on she lives in us just as truly as we lived in her before we came into the world. It's extremely singular. Every day now as I live my own life it's as if I were giving her a voice with which to speak. So, instead of saying to myself, 'This is what I feel, this is what is happening to me . . .' I think instead, with a sort of sad astonishment, but with joy too in the discovery, 'So this is what she experienced, poor soul, this is what she suffered.' We come together," she said. "We always do finally come together, but so late!"

Slightly crushed by this confidence, in which I saw, rather than a miraculous coming together, some sort of irksome interference with the personality and individual freedom, I began to speak against Grandmother in my turn.

"You scarcely resemble her at all, thank God. In the first place, you're a trotting horse like Grandfather. You're not in the least a stay-at-home. . . . And in the second place, you're not yet too quarrelsome. . . ."

She received my gentle teasing with a sidelong smile.

"That may come," she said, and began to defend Grandmother bitterly. "And anyway, she wasn't as quarrelsome as it is said. She became so when we all pushed her to the limit."

"How was that?"

"By resisting her love. There are two sorts of love. One closes the eyes and is easygoing. The other keeps the eyes open. That was her way, and it was exacting and difficult."

"But if it's true, as you say, that she loved Grandfather so much, how is it that in the long run she never completely forgave him for dragging her into the western adventure?"

"Simply because love finds it hard to forgive the slightest lack of love."

"And it was a lack of love on Grandfather's part to be determined to transfer his family at all costs?"

"Ah, I no longer know," Maman admitted. "Fundamentally they were both right. No doubt it's this that keeps us so far from each other in this life. There's always something to say on both sides."

"Really," I said, "if love and marriage are as you say, they seem to tend rather to diminish the human being. . . ."

"Diminish!" Maman exclaimed. "Then you can't have understood a word of what I've been trying to explain to you —that it's the only way, on the contrary, to get a little outside one's self. . . . But you're young," she said, with a sudden tender indulgence. "Stay young," she begged me, as if this were in my power. "Stay young and always with me, little Christine, so I won't become too old and quarrelsome too soon."

With one accord we burst out laughing. Then Maman turned her eyes back to the hills and I saw them fill with that joyous freedom the soul knows before it feels any need to possess, when the world and things offer themselves as if for the first time and to it alone. I understood somewhat better the attraction this road held for my aged mother. This freedom to receive everything, since no important choice has yet broached the possibilities, this infinite and yet at times troubling freedom must itself be youth. And no doubt it was upon this source of ephemeral freedom that Maman was still able to draw. Ah, no matter what she might say about human love and how much we learn from its restraints, I felt clearly as I watched her that it is only in solitude that the soul tastes release.

Then I heard her exclaim beside me, "How charming these hills are . . . and young, don't you think?"

"Young? I don't know. It is claimed, on the contrary, that they are extremely old formations. . . ."

"Oh you don't say!" she said, a trifle vexed, and went on chidingly, "You know, Christine, you ought to draw a map of these tangled roads, since you refuse to ask directions when you set out or on the way, saying that it's contrary to the spirit of the journey, that we must trust entirely to the road. That's all very well, but why couldn't you make a map of our little country? Otherwise, one of these days," she concluded on a note of rather tart reproach, "you'll end up by losing my Altamont road."

I burst into laughter. What melancholy and mistaken idea could I have got into my head! Maman was neither threatened, nor aged, nor diminished. At heart she was scarcely fifteen.

5

I had already heard at times the summons, insistent and alien—coming from no one but myself, however—that, in the midst of my games and my friendships, commanded me to set out to measure myself against some challenge, vague as yet, that the world flung to me or I flung to myself.

I had succeeded until then in freeing myself from this stranger. Then, without his speaking much more clearly, I began to hear him hounding me at every turn. (I say *he*, for how else can I name the one who became little by little my tyrannical possessor?) Were I for a moment happy in my heedlessness, my small reasonable plans for the future, I would hear his remonstrances again: Why do you put off going? Sooner or later you'll have to do it. . . . I was tempted to ask, "Who are you who pursues me so?" but I did not dare, for I knew that this foreign being within me, who was quite insensitive, if need be, to the sorrow he would cause to me and to others, was also myself.

Yet my life pleased me and my work as a teacher was high enough surely to fill it. Besides, I had my mother and she had no one but me.

And then this life I was living, as if it felt itself threatened, began to cover me with caresses and seemed more tender and precious to me than ever before. It is always when we love life that it loves us best in return, as if in a marvelous accord.

How well I remember that year of my life, the last perhaps when I lived quite close to people and things, not yet somewhat withdrawn, as happens inevitably when one yields to the intention to set things down in words. Everything still existed simply for me that year, because of the precise and reasonable duties that stitched me to life. It snowed, and quite artlessly I received the sensation of moist cold upon my cheek. The wind blew, and I ran to see from which direction it came. Our town was not an enigma to me, an invitation to lift up the roofs and see what was hidden within. It was a small town of friendly houses, whose people I knew, as well as all their habits, the hour at which they went out, where they went. I remained for some time at ease in life . . . not slightly to one side. Seldom since then have I been able to return completely to this or to see things and human beings otherwise than through words, once I had learned to use them as fragile bridges for exploration . . . and, it is true, sometimes for communication also. I became by degrees a sort of watcher over thoughts and human beings, and this passion, however sincere, uses up the insouciance that is needed for life.

For a short time longer, then, I knew the free play of my own thoughts—and do those who still possess it sufficiently realize their good fortune? They did not seem important enough for me to stop them in their tracks, impose a halt upon them, retain them, make use of them. Free still, they went their modest joyous way.

Now, as soon as they come to me, I fancy that they are for others, too, to some extent. I search them, work over them. In this way they have become a weariness to me.

———

Not much later, the sense and warmth of reality, to which I was attached as to my dearest possession, were taken from me and I have never dreaded anything as much since then as to see this deprivation recur.

I walked in our town and it had become as insubstantial and pale to my eyes as a cinema town. The houses on either side of the street were of papier-mâché, the streets themselves empty, for when passers-by brushed against me, I seemed scarcely to hear them come or realize that they had faces. When it snowed, I seemed scarcely to be aware that snow fell on me. I myself, moreover, was filled with a sort of emptiness, if it may be so expressed.

Sometimes a strange question rose from within me, as if from the bottom of a well: What are you doing here? Then I would cast my eyes around me. I would try to attach myself to something, familiar to me yesterday, in this world that was fleeing from me. But the troubling sense persisted that I was here only by chance and that I had to discover the place in the world, as yet unknown to me, where I might feel rather more at home. The thought, seemingly so trivial and yet disturbing, accompanied me everywhere: This is over. This is no longer your place. Now you are a stranger here.

One day, exhausted by all this, I tried to speak to my mother about what I was feeling.

"Maman, in your own life, have you sometimes had the impression that you are here by mistake, that you're a stranger?"

"Often," she said, as if projected by this simple question into that vast and terrible reverie where we are so alone with our own knowledge of ourselves. "Do you believe there are many people who are so satisfied with their lives that they never feel confined—or strangers, if you prefer?"

"You never let us know that you . . ."

"What would have been the good? You know that in my

youth I was eager to learn and travel and raise myself as much as I could. . . . But I was married at eighteen. My children came quickly. I haven't had very much time for myself. Sometimes even now I dream of an infinitely better person I might have been able to be . . . a musician, for instance—isn't that foolish?" Then she added quickly, as if to put me off the track, prevent herself from being revealed to me, "Everyone has such dreams—everyone, I tell you."

"If you had it to do over again, would you get married just the same?"

"Certainly. For I look at you and tell myself that nothing is lost, that you will do everything I wished to do in my place and better than I could."

"Then that compensates?"

"It does more than compensate. Haven't you understood yet that parents truly live over again in their children?"

"I thought you chiefly relived the lives of your own parents."

"I relive their lives and I also live over again with you."

"That must be exhausting! You can't have much time to be yourself."

"At any rate, it's perhaps the most illuminated part of one's life, situated between those who came before us and those who follow after us, right in the middle. . . ."

But all this, I thought, did not bring us to the subject I wished to broach.

"Listen, Maman," I said, "would you approve if I told you that very soon perhaps . . . ?"

"What do you mean? You're not also thinking of going away?"

"Yes, Maman, for a year or two."

She considered me for a long time, as if withdrawing all the while, withdrawing terribly from me. It was unbearable to me that, simply because I had told her I wished to go away,

I should see her go on ahead, retire first. Then she burst into vehement reproaches.

"So you're going away too. That's what you're plotting. I should have suspected it."

Even more disturbing to me than this sudden violence was the effort I could see her making to calm and control herself.

In a toneless voice she asked, "Going away? But where?"

"To Europe, Maman."

"Europe!" she repeated, the remoteness of this word renewing her indignation. "But why? Why? What will you do over there? In those old tormented countries, so different from ours."

"But that very difference, Maman, should be enlightening. Anyway, it's chiefly to France that I want to go."

"To France!" she cried, as if in scorn, she who had always spoken of it to us in a tone of the highest respect."

"Where else?" I said. "After all, I was brought up to believe that France was our ancestral country and that I'd feel perfectly at home there."

"Well, it's not true. That's the greatest of all the chimeras we've ever fostered."

"Perhaps so, but wouldn't it be better to go and see, before one says it's a chimera?"

"Oh you don't say!" she said derisively, then tried to compose herself, like one who perceives that there is a hard battle to be fought. "In the first place, if you want to write, you don't need to rush to the ends of the earth to do it. Our town is made up of human beings. Here as elsewhere there is joy to be described, sorrows, atonements. . . ."

"But to see it, shouldn't I first go away from it?"

"Go away! All my life I've heard those words! From the mouths of all my children! Where did you all get that passion for going away?"

"From you, perhaps."

"Perhaps—but I didn't go."

"Try to be reasonable."

"Reasonable!"

And she continued stubbornly, "A writer really needs nothing but a quiet room, some paper, and himself. . . ."

"Himself, that's just it."

"So to be yourself, you propose to break everything?"

Before the intemperance of our speech, our defenses fell for an instant and we looked at one another in grief.

"To think that only yesterday I believed you were happy," she lamented.

"Remember, Maman," I said, "if you and Grandfather discovered the prairie on your way west, it was because you'd first abandoned something."

"Would you dare to tell me that in order to discover you must abandon everything?"

"Some things, anyway. When you were younger you understood."

"Understood!" she cried. "Do you think one understands when one is young? Understanding is a matter of experience, of a lifetime. . . ."

"Well, since you understand everything better than I do . . ."

"That's right, turn my own weapons against me. Do you mean to wear me down as we all combined in the old days to wear down my poor mother?"

"You're beginning to be like her, as a matter of fact," I said unkindly, to which her only reply was a wounded look.

It was useless. She could not or would not yield to my arguments. And yet, pathetically, I continued to believe that arguments could be effective against a tortured spirit. We became to some extent enemies, my mother and I. She had the sorrow in her old age of holding hostile feelings against me. How could it be otherwise? When parents oppose their children, are they not often struggling against the audacity of their own youth, come back to harass them when they are tired out and through with adventure?

For almost a whole year Maman, incessantly vanquished, incessantly beginning again, faced the part of me that was most similar to herself as she had been, discouraging it with a bitter thrust, mocking at it, and sometimes, quite unexpectedly, pitying it.

Neither she nor I, during those cruel months, was attentive to the world and the seasons.

Sometimes, if I went for a few weeks without speaking of my plan or if I merely seemed to be interested in something else, she would draw some sort of timid hope from this. I would see her eyes watching mine, as if spying out the lie of the land, ready to flee at a moment's notice or become reconciled.

Spring came this time without her noticing it. She observed the renewal of life belatedly when it was already far advanced, almost complete. On an already warm day she raised her eyes in astonishment toward the sky and sighed, "Cléophas must have sowed his fields a long time ago. His fields . . ." she repeated, as if lost in a dream.

Then the summer was behind us. I was to leave at the beginning of October. I had booked third-class passage to Paris. From the depths of Manitoba to the City of Light, as I naïvely expressed it, is a great step. I trembled at the thought of embarking upon it now that the journey before me was taking on the appearance of certainty. I was beginning to dread that exhilarating moment of departure that is also the moment when we take our exact measurement in the world and find it so small that our hearts almost fail us. Yet this extreme vul-

nerability seemed to me then, and seems to me now, one of
the most necessary stages to self-knowledge.

Grandfather must have experienced it when he plunged into
the still savage territories of the west. Perhaps we were not,
after all, so far from each other—the pioneer heedful of the
call of a land still to be created and I, who heard, from a
young and half-formed country, the summons of the exacting
ancient cities.

Besides, it has always been like this in our family. One gen-
eration goes to the west; the next makes the journey in re-
verse. We are always in migration.

Maman was perhaps close to admitting that she felt herself
to be too old to lose me, that there is a time when one can bear
to see one's children go away but after that it is truly as if the
last rag of youth were being taken from us and all the lamps
put out. She was too proud to hold me at this price. But how
insensitive my lack of assurance made me. I wanted my mother
to let me go with a light heart and predict nothing but
happy things for me.

Sometimes she dared to offer me a word of warning, at
which I bristled.

"Perhaps you'll have a hard time there. What will you live
on?"

"My savings will be enough for a year . . . perhaps two.
After that, I'll manage."

"I'll be anxious," she said.

To which I replied, slightly provoked, "But why? There's
no need for you to be anxious."

Then a day came when I suggested, "Before I sell my car,
would you like us to make our trip to see Uncle Cléophas? On
our way back, we'll go by your Altamont road."

6

Just what was it that happened that day? The hills seemed to me less high, less shapely, almost insignificant. Was I so far ahead with my departure that I was comparing them already with the mountains I was to see, those mountains whose names I had been saying to myself since childhood—the Alps, the Pyrenees?

It's true that it wasn't really sunny that day and the autumn didn't glow as it usually did. The familiar colors were there, if you will, but subdued. At any other time Maman would have told me that this was through lack of frost, for at least one night of it was needed to put nature on the alert and make it assume its burning shades. But she said nothing. This was the most painful part of it, that we had to avoid almost all the subjects that had pleased us in the old days and keep to banalities. After a moment I turned toward her and saw that her face was creased with disappointment.

"These aren't our hills, Christine. You must have taken the wrong road."

"Still . . ."

"Our hills were closer together, more attractively grouped, higher too."

"We must have become accustomed to them."

"But the second time we passed through them, they still seemed charming, you remember."

"Well, perhaps we're only seeing them today as they've always been."

"Ah, do you think so?"

I had succeeded in shaking her, and she began to scrutinize the landscape with a doubtful expression that was pathetic to see. Just what was missing from our trip today? Something in the hills themselves? Or in the way we looked at them? In Maman's eyes, at any rate, I saw no return of that young and released expression I had observed on our previous trips. I already knew, of course, that remembered happiness does not come at our bidding, that it belongs to a different world from that of the will; but I was stubborn, I was determined that Maman should grow young before me once again.

"Still, these knolls are beautiful," I said.

"Perhaps, but they're not ours."

In a sense it was the same landscape we had traveled through and loved, but as if blurred. It gave us the same painful impression as does an imperfect photograph of a beloved face.

The mounds continued to slip past, without much spirit. A great shut-in heat prevailed between them. Maman finally granted them only a vague and slightly indifferent glance, as if she were quite prepared to lose everything now and indeed didn't much care. Now indifference is the one thing that all my life I have found it least possible to bear. I did not know that old people must have at least a trace of it, however, if they are to withstand the blow of seeing something taken from them each day.

"Maman," I said, "are you going to fall asleep right in the middle of the hills?"

She started, looked quickly around her and then, noticing a hillock that was a little higher and more shapely than the others, began to smile, not at this knoll perhaps but at something it suggested to her, something enchanting and young that came to her from far away but intact. Then her hope fell; her eyes grew dull.

She reproached me a little fretfully, "I told you you'd end up by losing my Altamont road."

Had I lost it?

In my mind I set about retracing my usual itinerary as well as I could. I passed again by the silent crossroads. Had I not hesitated at the first of them and taken a different direction from that of our previous journeys? How could I be sure? This Altamont road was like a dream—did I really know it? I had found it twice, chanced upon it, without searching. Was it not one of those roads one never finds again when one wills it too strongly? I had never, in any case, detected the least trace of it on the maps, though it is true that most of these maps do not take account of hamlets of less than ten houses or of the roads that lead to them. And meanwhile I was asking myself: Hasn't Maman aged enormously all at once? Will she even be able to wait till I am ready to show her what I can do? And if she is not, will what I am so anxious to accomplish have any value in my eyes?

Then I heard myself say in somewhat impatient tones, "What road do you think it is then, if it isn't the Altamont road?"

But was it another road?

Could there, in fact, be two roads into these hills where almost no one went any more—one lighthearted and happy, crossing the peaks, and another, lower down, which would skirt, but never enter, the little secret country?

Once again Maman began to scrutinize the sides of the road. She did it with a sharp but unhappy vigilance in which I believed I could distinguish a fear that she might no longer be able to recognize what landscapes had once had to offer her. Because she was too old now? Too weary? Because her memory was failing? Or her sensitivity? Because it was lost to her forever perhaps?

As on the previous occasions, we looked behind us for a moment as we emerged once more upon the plain. Against the already dark horizon no slightest undulating line of hills stood out, not even one of those clouds that imitate them so often in our Manitoba sky. But it was late, it is true; almost no light remained.

We reached those tall, bright yellow signposts on which the likeness of a buffalo appears. Once Lord of the Prairies, roving at will across these open spaces, now, on these metal plaques, he points out the main roads of Manitoba, which he maintains in the most direct line possible from town to town.

We had been rolling bumper to bumper along the monotonous highway for some time when Maman lifted her head and said defiantly, "No, Christine, that wasn't the Altamont road."

"How do you know?"

"Because we didn't see the village of Altamont."

"Such a tiny village," I said. "If we'd just chanced to look on the wrong side of the road while we passed it, we'd have missed it. You remember it's all on the same side of the road."

She seemed for a moment disconcerted and confused but almost at once began to search for arguments against me.

"I certainly looked at both sides of the road at once," she said.

Ahead of us, planted squarely on the prairie grass, loomed the cement factory, blanching and stifling everything with its chalky breath. Then came the new developments, identical cottages ranged sadly in long similar avenues on the edge of the ancient meditative plain. The young cities of my country have not had time yet to make themselves personalities to match the grandeur of the landscape that encompasses them. But it occasionally seems that the prairie is offering to our imagination these cities of tomorrow perhaps, ideal and in its own image, when it raises them on the rim of the horizon in mirages of marvelous completeness, perfectly in place.

"It's not your fault," Maman resumed, "but how sad it is that today of all days we should miss the Altamont road."

What did she mean by "today of all days"? Wishing to be kind and to atone perhaps for some momentary flash of joy, I said, calling her by her first name, as I did sometimes when I wished, I suppose, to bind her to me more closely and at the same time defend my young and unsure independence, "Next time, Eveline, I'll find your Altamont road. I'll come back from Paris. You'll always be an ardent traveler. We'll set out for Altamont together. When I have money, we'll take lots of other trips besides. Why shouldn't we go some day, for instance, and see the real family hills, in Grandmother's village in Quebec?"

She gave me then such a bitter, forlorn, and desolate look that I didn't dare go on. And perhaps it was not after all so important that she didn't see the Altamont road that day.

Immobilized by age and circumstances, she did not travel much more. When she did so occasionally, it was only to go to help one or another of her children scattered over this vast country. But was this really traveling? Was it even living, to wait and wait, alone in the depth of Manitoba, while I went in search of myself along the great roads of the world: to Paris, London, Bruges, and Provence; and also along the little roads, known to those who are unable to do without solitude, across another range of hills, for instance, to Ramatuelle in the Maures, and along the coast of Cornwall to Saint Ives and Tintagel?

I sent her postcards, with a few words scrawled on their backs: "Mother, if only you could see Notre-Dame of Paris . . ." "Kew Gardens on a day in spring . . ." "Mother, you can't imagine anything more perfect than Chartres Cathedral glimpsed from a distance across the plain of Beauce. . . ."

The waiting emptiness, the lonely, slightly poignant expanses of my own country had not returned to me yet to pluck at my heart. Nor did modest existences in small provincial cities greatly disturb as yet the intoxication of my youth. Moreover, to learn to know myself and to write was a far longer task than I had thought at first.

My mother replied with long patient letters, tender, meticulous, and deceitful, so deceitful. She assured me that she had plenty to live on, no longer having many needs or even, really, the desire to travel. Once only did she write to me about hills, and then about the earliest ones of her life, those that attached us to the memory of my grandmother. "When you return to this country," she entreated, "if you're not too far away, go and see them. They're not so far really from Montreal. You go to Joliette. Then you take a road that goes up . . ."

What a strange dialogue we exchanged across the ocean, I speaking of not much else besides my discoveries, my mother of such modest landmarks that they could not have moved me much at that time.

She approved of me now: "You were right to go. The winter has been hard. I see that you are discovering, discovering! It must be exhilarating! See all you can while you are in France and take as much time as you need. . . . Why yes, my health is good. . . . That cold I had is almost better. I found the story you wrote extremely interesting. . . ."

It was nothing compared to what I would do for her if only she would give me time. But I was always and forever only at the beginning. As yet unaware that it could never be otherwise on this way I had taken, I hurried, I pushed myself; years passed; I hurried, I continued to think of myself as being on the edge of what I wished to become in her eyes before I returned to her. And I am sure that my eagerness for what I would become hid all the rest from me.

My mother failed very quickly. No doubt she died of illness, but, as so many people do fundamentally, of grief too, a little.

Her capricious and youthful spirit went to a region where there are undoubtedly no more difficult crossroads and no more starting points. Or perhaps there are still roads there but they all go past Altamont.

A Note on the Author

Gabrielle Roy was born in 1909 in Manitoba, where her grandparents had pioneered and where her father worked for the government's Department of Colonization. Her first novel, *Bonheur d'occasion (The Tin Flute)*, set in a working-class slum of Montreal, was widely acclaimed upon publication in 1945. According to David Stouck in *Major Canadian Authors: A Critical Introduction to Canadian Literature in English* (also a Bison Book), *The Tin Flute* "first documented [a] profound change in French-Canadian life and brought Quebec literature into the mainstream of English-Canadian and international writing." Her other works in English translation include *Where Nests the Water Hen*, *The Cashier*, and *Street of Riches* (also a Bison Book), all of which have been compared to the writing of Willa Cather. Miss Roy died in Quebec City in 1983.